INDENTURED SERVANT

The Mystery of Elizabeth Spriggs

By Tecla Emerson

Indentured Servant
© 2022 by Tecla Emerson

ISBN: 978-1-7377615-1-8

Edited by P.F. Klyce

Cover Design by Katharine Sodergreen
sodergreen@aol.com

Page Design by Robert Henry
http://righthandpublishing.com

Printed in the United State of America
Published by OutLook Publications
Pub3000@aol.com

Dedicated to the three Murphy girls

... pardon the Boldness I now take of troubling you ... believe what I am going to relate the words of truth and sincerity ...

~ Elizabeth Sprigs, 1756

INTRODUCTION

Not so long ago, an unusual letter was discovered. It had been penned in 1756 by a troubled young girl. The letter was signed Elizabeth Spriggs.

According to her letter, she had been suddenly and unwillingly separated from her family in England. She had been kidnapped and sold into indenture. How this could have happened is one of the many mysteries that her letter presents.

In the letter, she pleads with her father to forgive her, (for what the letter never tells us), and to at least send her a bit of clothing. *"We are almost naked, no shoes nor stocking to wear."*

What could this young girl possibly have done to cause her father to allow this? She was literate, which is evident from her letter. This was uncommon in the 1700s, and most unusual for an indentured servant.

The story that follows has been pieced together from the bits of information that "Bitsy" reveals. It tells us what may have taken place over 250 years ago. It tells of the life of a privileged young girl who had been transported against her wishes to Baltimore Town. It was where she was introduced to a life she could never have imagined.

Maryland, Sept'r 22'd 1756

Honored Father

My being for ever banished from your sight, will I hope pardon the Boldness I now take of troubling you with these, my long silence has been purely owning to my undutifullness to you, and well knowing I had offended in the highest Degree, put a tie to my tongue and pen, for fear I should be extinct from your good Graces and add a further Trouble to you, but too well knowing your care and tenderness for me so long as I retain'd my Duty to you, induced me once again to endeavor if possible, to kindle up that flame again. O Dear Father, believe what I am going to relate the words of truth and sincerity, and Balance my former bad Conduct my sufferings here, and then I am sure you'll pity your Destress Daughter, What we unfortunate English People suffer here is beyond the probability of you in England to Conceive, let it suffice that I one of the unhappy Number, am toiling almost Day and Night, and very often in the Horses drudgery, with only this comfort that you Bitch you do not halfe enough, and then tied up and whipp'd to that Degree that you'd not serve an Animal, scarce any thing but Indian Corn and Salt to eat and that even begrudged nay many Negroes are better used, almost naked no shoes nor stockings to wear, and the comfort after slaving during Masters pleasure, what rest we can get is to rap ourselves up in a Blanket and ly upon the Ground, this is the deplorable Condition your poor Betty endures, and now I beg if you have any Bowels of Compassion left show it by sending me some Relief, Clothing is the principal thing wanting, which if you should condiscend to, may easily send them to me by any of the ships bound to Baltimore Town Patapsco River Maryland, and give me leave to conclude in Duty to you and Uncles and Aunts, and Respect to all Friends

Honored Father
Your undutifull and Disobedient
Child Elizabeth Sprigs

Source: Elizabeth Sprigs, "Letter to Mr. John Sprigs in White Cross Street near Cripple Gate, London, September 22, 1756," Reprinted by permission of the Connecticut Chapter of the National Society of Colonial Dames of America.

"… a further Trouble to you"
Letter, 1756

"Guinevere, you truly are a trial!" Bitsy's eyes flashed, the blueness matching the morning sky. Her stepsister glared. "There'll be trouble if you ride that horse and I'll take no responsibility for it." Bitsy's fingers tightened, her gloved hand tangling in Felicity's reins. Her eyes widened as Guinevere, her head held high, stepped up on the mounting stool.

"I'll do whatever I please," she spat, her foot missing Destiny's stirrup yet again. The fidgety young gelding danced about. Guinevere tossed back the red hair that had escaped from her bonnet, "besides, no one is here except Mother and a few house servants, all the others have gone to town. And if you, Miss Telltale, don't tell anyone, then who's to know?"

"They'll be back," Bitsy said. "Here, take her." She held out the reins that had kept Felicity still, "I'll ride Destiny." The gelding, as if hearing her, pawed at the ground.

"Well, I don't see why you should ride Destiny and I should have to ride that sorry old mare."

"Father is not going to like this one bit, you know that, and he'll find out and I'm supposed to watch out for you." Bitsy's eyes flashed in annoyance.

"Well, I'm four years older than you and I don't see why you should be watching out for me."

Bitsy ignored her comment and said, "We're supposed to share Felicity, you know that. Here," she said again, passing the polished leather reins to Guinevere, "you take her, and I'll wait for you."

"Well Miss Perfect, I know as much as you do about horses, and I can certainly control Mr. High and Mighty here. You just watch." Again, she tried to mount the skittish horse, but her foot slipped. The empty stirrup dangled at an odd angle.

"Guinevere, you've only ridden a few times and Destiny isn't trained yet."

Guinevere's foot found the stirrup and she threw her bulk up onto the back of the horse. His eyes opened wide, the whites glaring hugely in his chestnut brown head. He whinnied in protest and danced around trying to dislodge the inexperienced rider. The stable boy appeared from the depths of the barn. Sensing trouble, he ran towards the girls slowing as he approached the horses.

"Whoa," he said holding up a hand.

"And where have you been?" questioned Bitsy.

"I've just..." he began.

"Never mind we don't need you, go away. Leave us," she said, her annoyance biting off her words.

His eyes never left the big horse. "Your father..." he began, his eyes darting between the two.

"Go," said Bitsy again. "Leave us." Her annoyance difficult to hide. She had little use and even less patience with any of the servants.

"Ahhhgh," gasped Guinevere as the horse bucked, trying to throw his burden. The boy, shorter than Bitsy but confident, reached out to steady the horse.

"Go, I said," Bitsy's voice was sharp, with undisguised annoyance.

The boy dropped the reins. It was all that was keeping the prancing horse from bolting away. Free and no longer able to abide the heavy load, the horse turned and pounded off. His hooves thundered on the ground, making deep indentations, his intention no doubt to dislodge the rider. The reins tangled around Guinevere's wrists and hands; it was all that held her in the saddle. Destiny's hooves threw up clouds of powdery dust as he galloped off, Guinevere's screeches of protest driving him on.

"I told you," yelled Bitsy at the retreating figure. Throwing herself up onto Felicity's back she watched for just a moment as Destiny tore down the winding path, his passenger bouncing wildly on the awkward side saddle; her skirts billowed out in a tangle behind her. The pounding of the hooves echoed through the morning air as he bolted down the twisting path, through the field and on towards the copse of trees. It took Bitsy no time to steer Felicity down the trail. "C'mon girl, go," she said, ignoring the stable boy. She kicked her heels hard into the horse's side.

Destiny was far ahead of the mare. "Could she be a bigger fool?" she whispered as Felicity gained speed. "Go horse," she said, using the riding crop on the mare's rump. Unaccustomed to being struck, the horse leaped forward in surprise. "Go Felicity, we have to catch them." She knew she would never adjust to the awkwardness of balancing on the side saddle as she dug her heels into the horse's ribs.

"Good girl," Bitsy whispered close to the soft white ear. Holding herself low in the saddle, leaning forward, the coarse hair on the piebald's mane whipped against her cheek. Her bonnet flew off behind her, the ribbons fluttering through the air.

"Go girl," she said again, "we can't lose them or there'll be trouble for sure." She swatted at the mare's rump again. She could feel the horse straining unused muscles in an attempt to catch up. "There," she said pulling on the worn leather reins, "I see them."

The cloud of dust was like a beacon.

"They're heading for the lake. Careful girl," she said, pulling on the leather straps. Overhead branches threatened to sweep her to the ground. Destiny in a mad gallop had chosen the walking path that Bitsy and her father and their friends used when they had come to the lake for picnics. It seemed so long ago. Rarely had anyone taken a horse there. The trail was too narrow and overgrown with low hanging branches.

Felicity picked her way carefully around the roots jutting out of the hard packed earth, while trying to avoid the spruce and cedar branches that were reaching out like long grotesque fingers to block their way.

Trotting along the curved path, the lake came into view. Her heart jumped into her throat. The thick branches allowed only a shadowy light to poke through, but Bitsy could make out a heap of disheveled clothes piled in the middle of the narrow trail. Pulling up on Felicity's reins she squinted into the dappled sunlight. It looked like a huge pile of shiny pink rags with a pair of white stockinged legs sticking out, but there was no doubt it was her loathsome stepsister lying in a heap on the ground.

"Guinevere, I told you..." She pulled up on her horse and slid to the ground.

"Where are you hurt?" Fear and concern creased her forehead. "Please, Guinevere, speak to me open your eyes."

Guinevere moaned, then blinked, and tried to sit. She looked up into the rosy face of her younger stepsister. A bright red trail of blood oozed from a cut on the side of her forehead. It dripped from the ends of her red hair staining the front of her once fine dress.

"It's all your fault! You did it. You made me ride Destiny." Tears, more from exasperation then pain, streamed down her blotchy cheeks. She looked down at the front of her ruined dress. Ruined beyond repair. She began to sob. "Look what you've made me do."

"Guinevere, you know I've done nothing of the sort. Now hold still and I'll try to staunch that bleeding and get you home." Pulling back a hank of the blousy hair, she searched for the source of the trail of blood. "You'll be alright. Destiny was just trying to brush you off by running underneath those low branches. Stop blubbering and I'll try to get you up on Felicity."

"Oh, it hurts so. I'm going to die I just know it."

"Will you hush, you're not going to die. Here now, I'll wrap it," she said, ripping the ruffle from her own petticoat, "The bleeding will stop. Now hold still while I tie this."

As Bitsy could have predicted, Guinevere did not hold still but squirmed and sobbed and made it as difficult as possible.

"Hold still," she said again, trying her best to tie a tight bandage. "Now sit a moment and I'll find Felicity." The mare had wandered down to the lake for a cool drink. Destiny was there too but he'd have to wait; she'd deal with him later. Felicity came easily when Bitsy breathed out a low whistle. "Good girl," she whispered in her ear. "C'mon, you've got to take Guinevere back home," she said as she led the horse back to the trees.

Helping her stepsister up on a tree stump, she gave her a push as she tried to hoist her sweating body onto Felicity's back.

"Go on now, I'll try to catch Destiny and bring him back." As she spoke, she turned the mare in the direction of home and gently slapped her on the rump. "Go horse," she said.

Guinevere, hiccupping from her sobs, dried her mud-streaked cheeks with her sleeve. Horse and rider trotted off without a backward glance.

The lake waters were cool and still as she washed her stepsister's blood off her hands. Bitsy pulled out the carrot that she'd been saving for Felicity, thankful that she still had it.

"Destiny, come," she said, knowing he couldn't resist an undiscovered morsel. She held out the tempting treat, but catching Destiny was as difficult as Bitsy had imagined it would be. Riding him home would be even more difficult. He refused to stand still to be mounted. The best she could do was to lead him home, holding his bridle and repeating over and over calming and nonsensical words.

Progress was slow. The sky darkened as they made their way along the tree lined drive.

They'd been gone far too long. Clouds were forming on the horizon and a wind sprang up from somewhere in the north. Bitsy shivered. There was a storm coming to be sure. There would be rain before nightfall. As she walked the horse along the path to the stable, she lifted her eyes toward home. She was met by a frightening sight.

Reaching out a hand she twined her fingers in the horse's mane, feeling the warmth from his long sleek neck. Standing at the edge of the sloping lawn, hands on hips, cheeks flaming red and hateful eyes nearly bulging from a contorted face, stood her enraged stepmother.

*"... fear I should be extinct
from your good Graces"*
Letter, 1756

Bitsy's fingers plucked at the braided trim on the waist of her riding dress. She chewed on her lower lip as she stared at the face glaring down at her. Why? She nearly said it out loud. What had possessed her father to marry this person? He had met her at Court and knew she was well connected, but was that enough reason to bring her here, to their estate tucked back in the hills, away from the bustling city of London?

Urdeen, her new stepmother, had pulled herself up to her full height, and it was considerable. She stood, blocking the way; lips tightly pressed together, her eyes so often bulging were now dark slits. Bitsy stopped. She thought fleetingly that her stepmother must have once been mildly attractive in a plain sort of way, with her high cheek bones and large dark eyes, but now? She did have an unusual way of dressing, tending towards bright, almost garish colors with more lace and frill than was necessary.

Her favorite color was a shocking brilliant dark violet, more vivid than throbbing veins and not easily worn by most people in the bright sunlight of the day. And today this was the color she was wearing. What was astonishing was how her face nearly blended into the dress as her anger overwhelmed her.

"Elizabeth," she spat out. "You explain yourself at once. You've very nearly killed my daughter, you nasty child. You weren't content with killing your own mother, were you?"

Ignoring the look of horror that passed over Bitsy's face she continued, all the while shaking her tightly balled fist.

"Just wait until your father returns, there'll be the devil to pay, I can promise you that." She stomped her foot in a most undignified manner. "Take that horrid horse to the barn immediately. He is to be destroyed as soon as your father returns. I just don't understand what you have against my Guinevere," she persisted, her voice rising an octave. "She's been nothing but kind and thoughtful to you. It's no wonder you haven't any friends. Why, you'd try the patience of a saint, I do declare. And just look at you." She shook her finger. "Have you been rolling in the mud, perhaps? There's just no hope for someone like you. I don't know how your father has man-aged you all these years by himself."

Her shaking finger returned to a clenched fist. Not waiting for an answer, she whirled around, yards of shiny dark fabric becoming a blur as she stomped off to the huge grey stone castle-like house.

"But I didn't..."

"Now don't add lying to what you've already done," Urdeen said turning back. "Guinevere said you'd be telling tales to get out of this. I won't hear it. Just look at you, and look at your petticoat; my stars, it's ripped and dragging in the dirt. What have you been doing?" Exaspera-tion exuded from every pore. "Never mind," she said holding up her hand to ward off any further discussion. "I won't listen to any more of your lies. You just get yourself up to your room and cleaned up immediately and get that dreadful horse out of my sight."

Bitsy wondered once again, how was it pos-sible that this woman could be a distant cousin of King George II. That was the story anyway and one that her father had backed, saying it was either a fifth or sixth cousin. He had told his entire household staff that Urdeen's mother had kinship to the King. It came from the German side of long ago he said.

Regardless, she was now the wife of a country gentleman and responsible for a household staff and two daughters, only one of which was hers.

Bitsy knew that once again she would be held responsible for all that had happened. Guinevere had done it again. But Destiny. He wasn't to blame. Her wonderful horse. He was spirited and young, they all knew that. He'd soon be trained. She kept her fingers twined in the horse's wild mane.

"We've ridden together before, my friend, you're not bad or wild. Why does she say that?" She rested her forehead for just a moment on his warm neck; a lone tear trailed unchecked down her cheek. He was the most beautiful horse that they had on the entire estate.

"Father said maybe one day you'd belong to me." He'd almost agreed. He had said they needed to wait 'til the horse had been trained properly before deciding. But he had smiled when he said it, so she was sure he would be hers very soon. Bitsy wiped at a tear with the back of her hand. Rarely did she cry. It was a sign of weakness. It made her angry when tears would start. She was never going to be one of those girls who cried so easily - usually just to get their own way.

"Oh Destiny, she can't mean it. She doesn't even know you," she said as she brushed the hair out of her eyes, deep sadness creased the corners. "You're so beautiful. How could anyone want to destroy you?"

With one hand twined in his mane she led him to the barn, tossing the reins to the stable boy. "Take him and brush him and do it right," her anger spilling over.

The boy lowered his head, "Yes Miss," he said his eyes not meeting the young girl's as he led the horse into the stable.

Bitsy, her feet heavy, walked across the yard, she pulled open the heavy door, letting it slam behind her. The sound echoed up the stone stairway. In no particular rush, she climbed the grand staircase to the third floor. The door to her room opened easily. Jillie appeared magically at her side as she always did, ready to help.

"Oh Jillie, I'm in trouble again," she said, dipping her hands in the wash basin.

"And what now Miss?" Jillie's voice was quiet and kind. "It can't be too serious, can it now?" A questioning look crossed her normally happy face as she washed the dust and dirt from the hands of her young charge. She asked no question but helped Bitsy remove her riding dress and her ripped petticoat. The answers would come, she was sure of it. She handed her a damp cloth to clean her face and began to brush out the luxurious golden hair.

"Ouch. That hurts," she said.

"Well Miss, you've got briars and branches and leaves all in your hair. It'll take but a moment. Now just hold still a bit, it won't hurt. And you might want to tell me a little about what you've been up to"

There was no hesitation as she told Jillie of her morning ride. Tears flowed freely as much as she tried to hold them back.

"Jillie, I have no friends, nobody likes me."

"Now that can't be true Miss, why you have me."

"Yes, but I have no one else, even the servants don't like me. Why isn't father here? We used to have such wonderful times. He taught me to ride. When it was just the two of us, we'd spend the whole day together. We'd take the carriage and go to London for the week and enjoy it all so much. And now I'm in trouble again."

Her faithful servant sighed as she pulled the boar bristle brush through the curling locks.

"I declare," she said, searching for something else to chat about. "This hair is just like your momma's. She had the same mass of golden curls cascading everywhere. I'll tell you it was truly a full-time job to keep it tucked up and neat under her cap. I do remember how your father loved it so." Her eyes twinkled in the mirror as she looked at her young charge.

"Jillie, why did Father marry Urdeen?"

"To be sure," she said, "I couldn't tell you. Perhaps just the loneliness of all these past years." She sighed again. "You know it's going on sixteen years since your momma departed this earth. Maybe he thought it was time you had a mother. Maybe he was hoping you'd find a friend in Miss Guinevere. Who's to know what was in his head." Her voice lowered to nearly a whisper. "She surely isn't like your momma though; I can tell you that."

"Why doesn't she like me? What have I done? She's hated me since the day she arrived here and it's been over a year and I've tried, truly I have."

"Well, Miss, sometimes there's no accounting for the way people's minds work but it'd be my guess that perhaps you're in the way and maybe she thinks you're interfering between herself and your father, if you know what I mean." She turned her attention to the brush, cleaning out bits and pieces of debris from strands of the fine gold hair. "Mayhap she's more interested in promoting her own daughter. Pardon please," she said, as she pulled the brush through, one more time. "This surely t'isn't my business to be chatting on about."

"But I've done nothing but try to help her. She's so mean."

"Ah, to be sure. Perhaps they're not intending to be quite so disagreeable; maybe they don't mean it so. Sometimes I guess there's no accounting for others behavior. But then perhaps," she mused, "they're hoping all this will be theirs someday. Ah now there I go again, I've got to mind me tongue and not be quite so free with my thoughts."

"Jillie, I know my mother wasn't like that."

"Now Miss, I'll tell you, your sweet momma was the belle of the north country." Jillie picked up the wide toothed ivory comb and began to pull it through the mass of curls. "She was sweetness itself, why she was loved far and wide. From the first time your papa saw her at that Candlemas ball so long ago, he was head over heels for her." She paused, a far-off look passing over her old grey eyes. "I just about raised her myself you know. I was there the day she was born and from that day on your momma was practically mine 'til the day she departed this earth."

Bitsy loved hearing Jillie reminisce about her mother. She knew her only by the portrait that now hung in her room. It had been over the big fireplace in papa's library, but when Urdeen came into their lives it was quickly banished to some dark corner in the attic, that is until Jillie brought it down.

"Jillie, do I look like her?"

"Well now see for yourself," she said nodding towards the likeness hanging over the mantle, "that portrait could be you. Same high cheek bones, same large eyes, yours a bit darker blue perhaps and maybe your hair isn't quite as blonde, but the resemblance is quite remarkable."

"Then what was she like at my age?"

"Why, Miss, you know she was the most sought-after young girl in the entire county. Gentlemen were swooning over her before she was even sixteen. She ignored them all you know. She was interested only in riding out over the moors. Much like someone else I know." She paused and let a smile pass between them.

"She hated her lessons and did everything she could to escape. And as for all the suitors who came to call, she paid little attention. That is of course until she was about nineteen." She sighed. "Then she met your father at the ball and that was that. They were married within the year."

Jillie patiently combed away the snarls as she tried to make some sense of the mass of tangles in Bitsy's hair. "Then of course they had those ten years of bliss. During that time there wasn't all that much for me to do, you know. They traveled a great deal and what with my bad heart and all I stayed to tend to things here."

"Jillie, tell me again, did she really want me?"

"Ah Miss, I'll tell you, there wasn't a happier day in this household than the day they gathered us all in the great hall and told us the grand news. They seemed beside themselves with joy. It'd been ten years after all since they'd been married. They'd given up all hope of ever having a little one."

"Well, and sure enough," she continued, "they stopped traveling and your papa would barely leave her side. She looked just wonderful the whole time she was carrying you. She had roses in her cheeks and was just glowing with happiness."

"Urdeen said I killed her."

"Oh, now Miss, you know that's not true."

"Jillie, what happened?" The words were whispered. She knew full well the answer, but she still pondered over it.

"Miss Bitsy, you just plain came too early. No one was prepared. There'd been a dreadful winter storm of sleet and ice and a gale that blew down just about everything in its path. We had a time I'll tell you."

"Ouch," said Bitsy when the ivory comb tangled in the mass of unruly curls.

"Excuse me Miss, trying to get through some knots."

"Well, then, what happened?"

"Well now, we could hardly believe her time had come. Your papa was frantic. He wanted to ride out himself to find the Doctor. It was just much too early for her lying-in. Well and then as it happened," she said, "I was the chosen one." Sadness like a fleeting shadow passed over her old eyes. "They felt I'd know more about wee ones coming into the world than anyone else. And maybe I did. I'd been at a few births over time, but I'd never actually delivered one by myself."

She paused for a moment, taking a deep breath. "Well, with that storm raging there just wasn't a way that doctor was going to get here on time. Your papa carried your momma up those stairs and into their bedroom." She stopped combing and looked at the reflection of her charge in the mirror.

"It was on the west side of the house and the storm wasn't coming from that direction, so they hoped it'd be safe." Gently, she pulled the comb through the shiny curls. "No sooner had he tucked your momma in then there was a terrible gust of wind. It seemed to scream past the house. It tore out that old oak and it smashed the window in that room to pieces. Why it made the whole house tremble." She took a breath. Bitsy could see the sadness in her eyes.

"Your momma tried not to cry out and to be brave. But you could see the fear." She paused, a distant look clouding her eyes.

"That was when your papa picked her up again and carried her up another flight of stairs. He brought her here to this very room. Well, no sooner had he laid her upon that exact bed that you sleep on every night, than there you were. Tiny beyond description but yelling louder than any storm ever could." She sighed again.

"Your momma started to decline almost at once, I'm sorry to say. There was just nothing that we could do." She didn't mention to Bitsy the huge amount of blood that had been everywhere. There was not a way to stop whatever was causing her life to slip away. Jillie knew her Mistress and knew she wasn't going to make it.

"Your momma held you as long as she could; then your papa took you and put you in the cradle. You can't imagine the sadness. She was slipping away before our very eyes. There was just nothing we could do. The storm outside was raging and the doctor never made his appearance until late the next day." She sighed.

"Just before she died, she told your papa she wanted to name you Elizabeth after her mother. It was a sad day Miss, I'll tell you."

"Then tell me again why you called me Bitsy."

She took a moment to clear her throat, "Well, you were so small that they didn't think you were going to be with us for long. They were so sure you were going to follow your momma. Elizabeth just seemed too big a name for one so tiny. They started calling you "Little Bit" and soon enough it ended up as Bitsy. Why, Miss, we didn't even think you'd survive the night."

"And then Lizzy was my wet nurse?"

"Yes, indeed that's a fact. She had one of her own she was nursing and a big strapping girl like Lizzie surely had enough for two. It took a while but within a month we knew you weren't going to leave us. There was a stubbornness in you that kept you going."

"And father, what did he do?"

"Well now it was a long road for him. They'd been married over ten years you know."

"You said once that he didn't want to see me at first."

"That's a fact. It was up to me to tend to you. But once you started walking you became such a part of his life. You were like his shadow, and he loved you, you looking so much like your momma and all."

"But Jillie, why doesn't he like me now?"

"I wouldn't say he doesn't like you. I'd say he just needs time. He'll be alright. He's getting accustomed to a new way of life. When he returns from his trip down to the auction, he'll make everything right again, you'll see."

"Oh Jillie, I hope so, I miss him so," she hugged her lifelong friend.

Jillie pulled the comb through one last time then plaited the mop of hair into one long, neat braid hanging down nearly to Bitsy's tiny waist.

"Now Miss we've been chatting so long it's near dinnertime. I'll have Cook send your dinner up to you. Then we needn't bother the new

Mistress tonight. How'd that be?" she asked, her eyes twinkling.

"Thank you, Jillie. That'd be just fine. Papa will be home tomorrow and then everything will be right again." Jillie poked at the fire, trying to coax some warmth and light from the dying embers.

Bitsy looked out the window at the gathering storm clouds before Jillie pulled the heavy drapes closed, shutting out the night. Behind the drapes they could hear the wind picking up as it rattled the cold panes of glass. The rain that had threatened earlier was beginning to splatter against the windows.

"My being for ever banished from your sight ..."
Letter, 1756

Bitsy was up with the sun. Early mornings were the best. Almost no one was about. Many mornings she would walk outside in the grass, damp with dew, inhaling the fresh morning smells. If time allowed, she could escape down the long drive all the way to the main road. Today was cold but pleasant; with tiny shoots of green just starting to emerge. The dappled sunshine spilling through the bare branches held a promise of warmth to come. In the summer shade from the overhanging trees would keep the path cool, giving it a peaceful and protected feeling.

Puddles from last night's rain were still visible at the sides of the long drive and in the freshly made ruts. Someone had already been this way today!

The morning held such promise that she walked further than she had intended, forgetting the time. Realizing that she would most surely be late, she hurried back up the drive, avoiding the gouges recently made by a horse drawn carriage. Everyone in the household knew that there was a required attendance in the dining room by the time the old mantle clock struck nine; that was the time when her stepmother and stepsister made their appearance for breakfast.

Bitsy tried to pretend she didn't notice Mary who was limping down the walk trying to get her attention. She had once been the upstairs maid but now with her leg crippled by the gout, was assigned to help Cook.

"Miss, Miss," she called, "You need to hurry, they're at breakfast already." Her voice had forced cheeriness as she tried to get Bitsy's attention.

"Oh Mary, leave me be won't you, I don't need another nursemaid. Here," she said, take these." Bitsy handed her boughs of evergreen. "Put them in my room" Mary spread out her freshly starched white apron and collected the pieces of pungent smelling cedar.

"Yes Miss," she said and dropped an awkward curtsy.

Bitsy continued her walk up the drive, her pace quickening. Shaking the dampness from the hem of her dress, she entered the great room just as the serving girl was placing the cold meat and biscuits on Urdeen's gold-rimmed plate.

"And where, pray tell, have you been?" asked her stepmother, not taking her attention from the food that had been placed before her.

"Why, Mother," she said, feeling the word get caught in her throat, but it was the term that she had been instructed to use for the new Mistress of the house. "I've only been out walking, just to the road and back."

"I sent Mary to fetch you. Did you not see her?"

"Of course, I did."

"Well, then where is she?"

"She's bringing some things up to my room."

"Elizabeth, you needn't be quite so hard on the servants, you know." She paused, her knife in one hand, her fork in the other. "You knew our meal was served at nine sharp and here you are late again."

"I'm sorry Madam, I shall try to do better in the future." She slid into her seat and stole a look at the red headed girl, sitting across from her, slouched in her seat. Her stepsister's forehead was oddly discolored, and her left eye was nearly swollen shut. She was not attractive on the best of days, what with her puffy cheeks, her pockmarked skin and her overly large nose, but yesterday's accident had turned her almost into a ghoul.

For a moment Bitsy thought she was going to laugh. She bit the inside of her cheek so hard it nearly brought tears to her eyes. But then Guinevere caught her looking at her and stuck out her tongue. You're nineteen thought Bitsy – why don't you grow up? But she could do nothing; Urdeen's piercing gaze would not leave her. Guinevere deserved that bump on the head for telling lies, she thought. Bitsy lowered her head, letting her escaping curls fall over her eyes.

Urdeen interrupted her unkind thoughts, "And so young lady, your father will deal with eliminating that rogue of a horse later. And he's decided to send you away for a while until you can learn better how to behave yourself."

"What are you saying?" Bitsy looked up shocked into disbelief. She had not been listening to her stepmother's lecture. "Is my father here? Is he here now?" The ruts in the drive must have been his returning carriage.

"He most certainly is and very disappointed and upset with you, I might add. He arrived quite late last night after the entire house had been shut up and all the servants in bed." She reached for another scone from the silver filigree basket.

"I was able to speak with him only briefly. He needs his sleep, as he traveled all night. He has said he'll deal with you at dinner." She continued slathering a huge amount of butter on the crumbling scone. She had been corseted so tightly that Bitsy thought she might just burst out over the top of her gown. It was a style that they were wearing at court and Urdeen was convinced that one day they would be invited back. It would be prudent she said to be ready when the invitation arrived.

Bitsy tried to steady her voice. "My father wouldn't send me away and he wouldn't destroy Destiny. You're lying just like your daughter."

"Best you watch that tongue of yours, young lady, and do not ever raise your voice to me or I shall be forced to report this scene to your father, and I do not wish to trouble him further." She used the blunt point of her butter knife for emphasis. Did they do that in the King's court Bitsy wondered as she rose from the table?

"It's not true. I hate you!" Bitsy said as she slammed down her linen napkin. The crystal goblets clattered against each other.

A thunderous look passed over her stepmother's face as she half rose from her chair, "Elizabeth, you get back to this table this instant."

"I shan't and you can't make me."

Bitsy, shocked by her own outburst, dashed from the room, tears stinging her eyes. Her feet hardly touched the floor as she flew through the door, slamming it hard behind her. There was no place to go except to the stables. Urdeen wouldn't follow her there. She hated horses, all of them. It was said that once she'd been thrown when she was a very young girl and since then had stayed as far away from them as she could. Even carriage rides frightened her. She rarely left the estate.

Not waiting for the stable boy, Bitsy grabbed one of the hard leather saddles, the weight nearly knocking her to the ground. She threw it on Destiny. "We're going for a ride, my friend, a long ride. They won't hurt you if you're with me and they'll never find us." With the back of her hand, she swiped at the tears flooding her eyes.

The horse turned to her and whinnied, nuzzling against her with his velvet nose. She tightened the cinch around his middle and climbed up on the stool. Placing one foot in the stirrup she threw her leg over his back. "We'll just leave that side saddle for Miss Prissie," she said as she guided the dancing horse to the door.

Destiny needed no urging. He was as excited as any young colt could be. He was out the door in a flash and racing towards his freedom. Needing no guidance, he galloped down the path. They moved as one, horse and rider, galloping across the dew-soaked fields. The morning air crisp and clean. Destiny chose his own goal and headed then into the familiar stand of trees and the peacefulness of the forest.

He chose his path going at a full gallop. Bitsy hung on, her knuckles white. She was exhilarated by the freedom, loving the wild speed. The horse galloped on through the trees, Bitsy bent low on his back, ducking to avoid the overhanging branches. Her hair streamed out behind her in long wavy tendrils.

The lake came into view. Destiny was lathered and panting, his sides heaving as he slowed his pace. Bitsy's heart was racing, pounding in her ears.

That was wonderful, she thought. She slipped off his back. Taking his bridle with one hand together they walked slowly back and forth along the edge of the lake, giving him time to cool.

"We'll think of something," she said. "They'll never find you." She patted his long sleek neck. He whinnied softly as if understanding. Pulling off her riding boots, she put them to one side. Destiny needed to walk more. He needed to cool completely. Moving slowly along the side of the lake she let the cold mud squish between her toes.

Destiny was content walking by her side, stopping now and again to take a sip of water. His breathing became less labored as he munched quietly on the new grasses just emerging in the late winter sun.

"Here, Destiny, my friend," she said looping the strap around a branch, "Stay here, there's grass and water; I'm going to sit in the sun and think of a plan for us," she paused, "one where they'll never find us."

She sat at the edge of the lake, resting against the base of a young tree. Dipping her bare feet in the cold water she watched as the ripples scattered and spread, moving gently across the quiet surface, disappearing in the distance. She needed a plan. Lying back in the damp grass, her hands beneath her head, she stared up at the few grey clouds. The light breeze was pushing them through the morning sky to some unknown destination.

Soaking up the warmth from the sun she let her eyes close as she slipped into a troubled sleep.

"Hey there, you girl, get yer'self up. Yer'

comin' with me."

Bitsy squinted up into the early afternoon sun. She shook her head trying to rid it of the drowsiness. She hadn't realized she'd nodded off; she'd only meant to close her eyes for a moment. The toe of a man's mud caked boot was poking her in the ribs.

She sat up quickly, shading her eyes with her arm. "Who are you? What do you want?" she asked moving away from his grubby boot. "You're trespassing on my father's land." Her voice rose with indignation.

"Get up, girl, and don't talk to me about yer' father's land. Yer' comin' with me."

"I will not!" She struggled to stand. "I'll not go anywhere with you. Who are you? Get off this land."

Standing tall and straight, anger flared in her dark blue eyes. Holding her hand up to block the afternoon sun, she looked more closely at the big man. "I know you!" she said in sudden recognition, "You're the gardener that my stepmother brought with her." The deep scar running from his eye all the way to his chin and the unkempt black hair made him easily recognizable.

He laughed. "Gardener, now, is it? Is that what she told ye?" He laughed again, a deep cynical laugh. "Whatever, I answer to many callings. Git up now in that wagon," he said, making a grab for her arm.

"I'll do no such thing," she declared, her chin rising defiantly.

"Alright then I'll do it meself." He wrapped a burly arm around her waist and easily swung her over his shoulder. He carried her to the wagon like a sack of freshly cut wheat. Her protests caught by the wind.

"What are you doing?" She beat on his back with her closed fists, her legs kicking out. "Put me down you brute, this instant."

"Ah now stop yer' strugglin', ye'll be put down in a moment." With that he dropped her, skirts tangled about her legs, still sputtering her protests, into the wagon piled high with hay.

"Ye'll excuse me, young Miss, I really don' have the stomach for this sort of thing, but these be me orders." Taking a filthy rag from his trouser pocket, he tied it tightly around her mouth, shutting out her protests. He bound her wrists and ankles with twine, struggling to keep her still. The roughness dug into her flesh, breaking the skin. Her eyes were wild, and her thrashing made it difficult for him to hold her. He tied her hands to her feet to further immobilize her and then threw handfuls of hay over her.

"There now keep still or ye'll be getting' a thrashin' from me own hands," he said, breathing hard and wiping at the sweat that was dripping off his forehead. "We've a-ways to go, so it'd be my suggestion that ye lie still and enjoy the ride." He threw still more hay on top of her. "The Madam said ye'd be a handful, but I told her I could handle it, ye bein' just a slip of a young thing," he said. His laugh, filled with scorn, cut through the brightness of the day.

He was hesitant and cautious but approached Destiny, holding out a reward of a carrot if he'd come closer. It was easy enough to grab his reins when he accepted the treat. He led him into the forest and tied him securely to a tree. It was deep in the gloom where he wouldn't be seen. There'd be time to deal with him later.

Climbing back up onto the wagon, he slapped the horses with the reins. "Now get on both a' you's. A sorry business this is when yer own family don't want ye." He spit over the side. "But I'll do me job." Wiping the spittle off his whiskers he continued his mumbling. "There's a shilling in it fer me the Mistress said. Go on now, Bess," he said, snapping the reins, "Go on

Freda, we've a ways to go before the sun rises tomorrow." He slapped them again. Picking up first one tired foot then the other the animals moved off, the clip clopping of their hooves echoing through the trees.

The old farm wagon creaked its way out to the main road as the afternoon sun began its descent into the western horizon. The unwilling passenger, exhausted by her struggles, had succeeded only in digging herself deeper into the prickly straw.

The sound of approaching hoof beats made her suddenly alert. She heard an all too familiar voice call out. "Whoa there, Foster. Hold up."

"Cain't Sir, promised the Mistress I'd get this load o' hay down to her sister's 'fore nightfall."

"Well then," he yelled over, "just tell me this, do you know the whereabouts of my horse Destiny?"

"Cain't say's I do, Sir. 'Been out in the field most of the day."

"Oh Father," she silently cried, "Is this what you intended for me? I'm sure not. If you'd only talk to me." Tears stung at her eyes. The rag tying her mouth closed, cut into her flesh. She struggled in vain; she was too far down in the pile of hay to be noticed.

"Well thank you then," her father called out.

This can't be, she thought, ignoring the one lone tear that slipped down her inflamed cheek. How could this have happened?

Curling up into a ball, she laid in the scratchy bed of hay. The rickety farm wagon continued on its course through the late afternoon and into the long dark night. The rhythmic clop, clop of the horse's hooves and the swaying of the wagon lulled her into an exhausted and fitful sleep.

Bitsy woke before the sun was up, hardly remembering where she was and what had happened. The wagon had stopped. The man dug down into the hay, his filthy hand searching her out. He grabbed her arm. An iron grip clamped around her wrist, as he pulled her out from under the straw. Bending to cut her loose, he stopped, took a closer look at her mass of cascading golden hair. "That's going to have to go," he growled, fingering some of the curls. "I believe that'll bring me a quid or two when I get to town." A glint of light reflected off the metal blade of his knife.

Bitsy closed her eyes tight as the blade slashed and cut and chopped off her hair. She dared not move at the risk of being slashed. When the butchering had ended there was a deep pile of hair lying on the wagon bench.

"Now Miss, I'll be unbinding ye," he said, stopping to spit into the dirt. "These be the rules 'fore I remove that tie about yer mouth. At yer esteemed stepmother's orders yer to be sent across the sea to the Colonies. You have, I'm told by the Madam," he laughed a deep cruel laugh, "disgraced the family." He spit again.

"They want nothin' more to do with ye. 'Tis said ye tried to murder yer sister and came mighty close to doin' the deed." He laughed again, a frightening sound. "I'm to secure passage for ye in whatever way I can and ye, my little sweet, are not to return ever again. Now young Miss if you agree to keep yer head about yerself, I shall unbind ye. Is that agreed?" His black eyes bored into her.

Bitsy looked at him in disgust and disbelief. She looked once more at his huge knife and sighed, resigned to her fate. She nodded her head in agreement.

His clumsy fingers struggled to remove the rag from around her mouth.

"How dare you," she sputtered, barely able to speak, surprised at her own outburst, "My father would never..."

"Miss, this be fair warning," he said clamping a filthy hand over her mouth and grabbing her arm. "Me instructions is that if ye don't go peaceable I'm to use whatever means necessary to dispose of ye in some other way. Now don't make me job harder." He shook her with the hand that clenched her arm, emphasizing his words.

Bitsy looked into the man's cold face; it was a face that looked as though it had been chiseled from stone with its deep lines and lifeless eyes. Yes, she was quite sure he would find some other way of "disposing" of her.

Rage boiled up inside her, but her tongue was frozen in silence.

"… my long silence"
Letter, 1756

"Ah now don't be puttin' on airs with me. Yer jus' like the rest of us." The words spewed out of the dark cavern of a toothless mouth. "Why look at ye. Not a farthing to yer name, not even a pair a shoes on yer feet. I do believe yer in worse shape than the likes o' me." The old hag stared with her one remaining eye at the bedraggled girl.

Bitsy had been on the prison ship for over two weeks and she was quite certain she did look very much like the rest of the motley "passengers."

"What were yer in fer, girl?" the woman lisped, spraying spittle like dew drops in a fog.

Bitsy chose to ignore the question and to ignore the old woman, much like she'd tried to ignore all the stinking bodies jammed together. She moved away from her inquisitor and closer to the edge of the crowded hold. When they had departed the port in London they couldn't have squeezed in another body if they'd all stood upright. After a week on the storm-tossed sea, close to twenty had already died, their remains thrown over the side with careless disregard. It freed up a bit more space for the rest of the "passengers."

Bitsy had remained mute since arriving at the ship. The turn her life had taken was beyond enduring. The reeking mass of humanity that had been thrown together was far removed from anything she ever could have imagined. Disease ran rampant through the group. Nights were filled with coughing and groaning and other sounds of suffering. Smells beyond description permeated every nook and cranny. Even the wood on the sides of the ship stank, having absorbed the foul odors of its passengers. It was hard to even take a breath in the fetid air.

Now, after almost two weeks of confinement they were to be herded to the upper deck for an airing and for water to be thrown over them. A bath it was called.

Bitsy, following the stinking mass of bodies, climbed up the rungs of the ladder. Emerging from the dank hold she raised her eyes and squinted at her surroundings. They had not been allowed on deck since boarding the ship.

The brightness of the early morning sky, after the dark confinement for all the many days, stung her eyes, causing tears to slip out.

The sails were taut, billowed out by a strong steady breeze. The vast expanse of ocean was all that could be seen on all sides of the little ship. Bitsy inhaled the clean ocean air, the saltiness giving it an unfamiliar but wonderful smell. Squinting into the bright sky, she pushed what was left of her chopped off hair back behind her ears. The day was perfectly clear with nothing more than a light wind. The ocean was an endless expanse of inky blue with sparkles of sun bouncing off the waves.

Her shipmates squeezed around her, everyone trying for a breath of fresh air. It was horrifying to see them in the light - all sizes, and all manner of society's misfits. She withdrew, trying to make herself smaller as she looked about her. Many of her shipmates were grisly characterizations of what the world's mass of humanity truly looked like. A boy, younger than she, dangled a misshapen arm at his side, one eye sunken, the eyelid permanently closed. A woman who may once have been pretty had the scars of the pox carved into sunken cheeks. She dragged one leg as she walked, the foot turned out at an awkward angle. An old man, with not a hair on his head or his body, was not only missing all but one tooth but an ear, leaving an odd hole in the side of his head.

Many others were scarred by past diseases and badly disfigured by who knew what. There wasn't a full set of teeth among them. Some were pitifully old and others pitifully young. Most were so poorly clothed they could be considered almost naked. What horrible crime could some of these young ones have possibly committed to have gotten themselves thrown in the gaol?

"Ha, ha, would ya' look at that pretty little morsel."

Bitsy, shrank further into the crowd, knowing one of the crew was pointing at her. "Why, mate, she's even got pearly white teeth. Now, have you ever seen the like?" Bitsy moved further into the center of the group. Standing taller than most, she hunched herself over and disappeared into a group of young boys.

The sailors quickly lost interest, turning their attention to the older "ladies." Laughing uproariously, they poked and prodded the women. One, taller than the rest, her head shaved for whatever reason, her arms hanging out of her rag of a dress, showed bruises and long welts from her wrists to above her elbow. "Go on with ya'," she said to the sailors. "Leave us be, ye nasty jack-tars."

"Aye. You talkin' to me?" He squinted up his eyes at her. She spat at him. Bitsy turned away as he raised his cat-o'nine-tails, wincing as the woman's scream tore through the air.

The sailors soon lost interest in their sport. They were tired of throwing water on the shivering bodies and were done with their exchange of ribald comments with some of the "ladies." Abruptly they ended the prisoner's time on deck and all the dripping trembling bodies were herded, much like wandering sheep, back into the hold. The women held what was left of their clothes close to their bodies, shielding themselves from the bold stares of the laughing sailors. One, who they'd heard called Jacques, tried to pinch or slap each as they walked by. The women held their tongues fearing the lash of the whip.

Locks and chains were no longer necessary. They had been removed as soon as the ship had gotten out of sight of land. None of the crew cared if they fought among themselves or even if they jumped overboard, which was highly unlikely as none could swim. It was hard to imagine that life in this crowded hell hole was better than the life most had come from in London's prisons. There were enough floggings with screams echoing over the waves that the "passengers" were reluctant to cause any trouble.

Bitsy held tightly to the rungs as she lowered herself down the ladder, ignoring the pushing and shoving. Without warning, a body from above was shoved into the hold. Arms and legs flying, it crashed down on her. Bitsy lost her grip, falling the last few feet. Pushing at the person on top of her to no avail she yelled "Get off me." Her voice was raspy with disuse. She shoved at the body crushing her chest.

"Blimy," said the body trying to right itself, "Those bloody jack-tars. They're worse than any blokes I've run into in England. Stop pushing at me, girl," she said to Bitsy. "You think I wanna be settin' on a bag o' bones like you? Get outa my way now."

"Out of your way?" said Bitsy, her voice spitting fire. She gave the girl one last shove.

"Well, I never," said the girl trying to right herself, one hand clinging to the ladder. Bitsy scrambled up and brushed at what was left of her once fine riding habit. She looked at the girl who had nearly broken her ribs. The girl was all fire and sass, her hands held up ready for trouble to either deliver or fend off a blow.

Shorter than Bitsy and as slender as a piece of well-worn rope, she had full, dimpled pink cheeks that gave her a cheery look, belaying the leanness of her frame. Her hair, a mass of deep red curls, was flying in all directions. Bitsy fleetingly wondered if she'd ever seen a comb. Irish rabble, she thought and turned to reclaim her corner in the bow of the ship. The girl scowled and gasped. Bitsy was still close enough to grab her as her ankle turned and she started to collapse. "Now what?" asked Bitsy.

"I do believe me ankles gone." The girl winced as she tried to put weight on her twisted foot.

Annoyed, Bitsy pulled at her arm, "Well dang," she said, surprising herself with her new guttural language, "you'd best come along with me, or you'll be trampled for sure."

Limping and eyeing her suspiciously, the young girl allowed Bitsy to lead the way. She leaned heavily on the offered arm.

"Come up into the bow," Bitsy said, not entirely happy with this new burden. "We're out of the way. We don't get as much to eat up there and we feel the waves a bit more but it's a little cleaner and quieter."

"I guess I didn't move meself fast enough for the likes o' 'em." The girl gestured towards the ladder.

"It's a sorry bunch," said Bitsy. "Come and sit and get off that ankle for a while 'til it mends," she said, realizing how alone she had been. "I'm Bitsy," she said as her manners returned - if just for a moment.

"Well now Bitsy, they call me Milly. You don' sound like one o' this rabble. What are ye doin' here?"

"I'm not sure myself," Bitsy answered in a low voice.

"And why is it you don' know?" Milly looked more closely at her.

Bitsy had no answer but let out a long sigh.

"We're headin' for the Colonies," she said. "You must know that much. We'll be sold into indenture when we get there for sure. Some o' this rabble has already been paid for."

Bitsy, nearly at a loss for words, eyed her new friend with disbelief creasing her forehead. "You can't mean it," she said. "Sold! What do you mean sold and to whom, pray tell?"

"Why to whoever wants us, would be me guess. Most o' this riffraff was released from prison. It's merry old England's way of gettin' rid o' the undesirables." She made an attempt at a half laugh, but it stuck in her throat and came out more as a choking sound.

"'Tis better than being a slave," she said. "Now if that were me fate, I'd jump overboard now. We're at least treated a mite better. After a few years they release us and we're off on our own to do as we please."

"Milly, you can't be one of the prisoners."

"Oh, my stars yes, indeed I am. I would've done anything they wanted to get out o' that hell hole, excuse me. Me Mum would not like hearing me speak that way if she was close by."

"Why were you in there?" asked Bitsy as she scratched at some unknown creature. It was crawling through her close-cropped hair.

"They say I stole a loaf o' bread. Ha!" She wiped a hand across her damp forehead. "It happened some months ago," she said looking over at Bitsy. "Me Mum was laid low, and all the wee ones was about to starve. T'weren't a morsel left in the cupboard. Me being the eldest, I had to do something." She coughed a raspy cough and wiped at her mouth with the back of her hand.

"I was making me way down the street," she said, "mindin' me own business and there was two loaves o' fresh bread, that I was sure fell from heaven above, but in truth fell off the back o' the baker's cart. One loaf was very nearly in the horse's dung. Well, I didn't think the baker'd even noticed so I made a dash for both o' 'em. I mean if not me, someone else most assuredly would've." She shrugged her bony shoulders. "I wrapped 'em up in me apron and ran. Sure enough there was a constable who saw the whole thing. I was thrown in the dungeon like some common thievin' scoundrel. Me family never even had any of the bread that I was thrown in prison for stealin'." She sighed.

"How perfectly dreadful. Will you ever get home again?"

Ah now I don't think that'll be possible. Me family by now is either dead or have moved on, maybe back to Ireland. They couldn't have lasted long in the condition they was in."

"Why did you come to England?"

"Me Pap." She was taking time to rub at her swollen ankle, wincing now and again, but continued. "Me Pap, he wanted a new life. There be eight of us, countin' me. Mam popped out another babe every two years. Soon's she was done nursing one there'd be another. I had seven younger sisters. Had a brother once too, but he died."

"How terrible," said Bitsy. "But why England?"

"T'weren't that far away. Me Pap really wanted to go on to the Colonies but how could we all get there? He wanted to learn how to work the sea."

Bitsy looked at her, a question in her eyes.

"He wanted to fish. Not much fishin' goin' on back in Ireland. He'd always been a farmer, just like his Pap, but he wanted something more. He hoped one day to get to the Colonies and to have his own fishin' boat."

"Where is he now?" asked Bitsy.

"Lost at sea he was," she replied. "First time out too. It was on a fishin' boat. They never came back. We watched and waited but they was lost at sea." There was sadness etched around her eyes, but she continued. "Mam took it hard, wanted to go back to Ireland on the next boat but there was no money 'cept the little I brought in and one of my sisters. We cleaned houses sometimes. When we could get hired," she said by way of explanation. "T'weren't that much work out there."

Bitsy tried to fathom the life that Milly must have come from and could barely imagine such poverty. Thoughts of the hired help in her own house pricked at the edges of her con-science. It was hard to imagine how life on this prison ship could be any bit better than where they had all come from.

"Me dream has always been to go to get to America. Didn't imagine it would be this way, but here I am. Passage is free, just have to work a few years, then I do what I want."

"And what is it that you want?"

"Land! I want me own home. I don't want to be someone's tenant or labor on for someone else. I want something to be mine and only mine."

"I've thought of that too," mused Bitsy. "Someday I want to raise my own horses and maybe have an entire farm ..." her voice trailed off. The two slipped into an uneasy silence as they stared off into the mass of stinking bodies; wanting to dream but feeling all of their hopes dashed, much like the breaking waves crashing over the bow, with water scattered everywhere, settling nowhere.

Over the next few days Milly and Bitsy be-came allies in the struggle for survival. Milly was skilled at snatching food that was thrown down to them. Bitsy knew that Milly was the only reason they didn't starve to death. She tried to help by taking their two cups and filling

them with water from the barrel that was lowered down to them. Most of the others would
struggle and fight for bread while she'd scoot
around the crowd and dip their cups into the
nearly fresh water, then, trying not to get jos-
tled would bring them back to the bow.

They had become quite skilled at their tasks
and had fallen into a quiet routine and then after what must have been weeks, a voice from
above yelled "Land ho!"

It was a sultry morning with little wind;
they had made almost no headway. For the past
few days, the sails had hung limp. The hatch
cover was thrown back as a grizzled old sailor, a
black eye patch covering one eye, yelled down,
"Git yer bony bodies up here."

With little hesitation the mass of stinking
decrepit bodies scrambled up the rungs of the
ladder, looking much like a teeming, crawling
bunch of cockroaches. Emerging for their "bath"
of seawater, most covered their eyes from the
brilliance of the bright sunlight. Peeking out
from shaded eyes, they had their first glimpse of
their new home.

Far off in the distance they could just make
out the land. It looked like a strip of horizon
that had been painted with a fresh coat of

green. It could be seen on both sides of the ship. They were in the Chesapeake Bay, so said the sailors. The joy felt by the passengers and the crew was hard to hide. It would be just two more days 'til they would arrive in Baltimore Towne.

"We made it," said Milly, "Can't say the same for many of them others." She sighed and squinted into the distance, her hand shading her eyes.

Bitsy stood listening for a moment to the sounds of the ship. "They lost so many," she said, "Don't they care?"

"I imagine so, after all it's money they coulda' had, but they pack us in so tight knowing some won't make it. Did ye not notice how much more room we've got? It's like we've got our own quarters now. I can actually stretch out me legs when we sleep, 'specially since that man King died."

"That wasn't his name," said Bitsy.

"I know that to be sure but look how he slept. He took all of his space and most of ours and told us it was his right. Too bad the scurvy didn't give a care if he was King or pauper. Sickness, me Mam always said, is what makes us all the same in the end - takes the rich and poor alike, doesn't care who you are."

"But so many dead," said Bitsy shaking her head, "And some so young. That little boy, re-member, the one missing his front teeth. Think he was Irish, but he never spoke. Thought he was going to make it but after his mother died it seemed that the light went out of his little eyes."

They knew that the number of passengers had dwindled to almost half. Most had died of disease, but others died of starvation and some just died from despair, they gave up and stopped eating and let themselves sink into oblivion.

Children had been the first to go, and then the older men began to succumb. Each morning the passengers were greeted with more bodies that had to be lugged up the ladder and then without ceremony deposited over the side. The dead were sent to their eternal resting place with only the briefest of words as scripture was read over them. They were placed on a plank and then dumped into the cold dark sea.

"I can't imagine how any of us survived this," said Bitsy looking around at the horribly pinched faces and vacant eyes of those who were left.

Milly scratched at the flea nibbling at her ankle, "It's been near four months; don't know how you and me got through."

"It was your skill at finding food," said Bitsy, smiling a tired smile. "Now what?" she asked, not sure if she wanted to hear the answer.

"Hard to know," said her friend, "but I'm sure it's not gonna' to be good."

"… unfortunate English People"
Letter, 1756

The docks were teeming with more people than Bitsy had ever seen, busier even than London on market day. It was early morning, near the first of June, and the town was just coming to life. The winds had not been favorable and the ship had struggled to get up the Bay, the two-day voyage becoming four. The cargo of people stood at the railing, watching, their tongues tied in either fright or awe as they looked at the place that was to become their new home.

"C'mon," yelled the sailor, his long stick prodding the slow pokes. "Get a move on," he snarled, "Or we'll dump ye' overboard for the fish to eat."

It was a sorry looking group that paraded single file off the ship and down the gangplank, their legs wobbly and shaky, their gait unsteady.

Two crusty sailors who couldn't resist, took one last turn at tormenting the motley group with slaps and pokes. Bitsy smacked at the hand that pinched her bottom, but it only seemed to encourage the toothless seaman. "I'll be seeing you again," he threatened with a wink. Milly swore at him, which brought a smile to Bitsy's face. She'd never heard words used quite that way before and was sure if she'd ever said such, she would have promptly been dispensed to the nearest corner. But that was before ...

"Help," screamed Milly. Bitsy turned and gasped. Milly had slipped, or more likely been pushed over the edge of the gangplank. Her friend was splashing and flaying in the water. Screaming with a high-pitched, terrified shriek, she went under, her head bobbed back to the surface, and she went under again.

"Help her you lunatics," yelled Bitsy. She yanked the prod from the hand of the sailor who'd been tormenting them so. Laying herself flat over the edge of the dock she yelled down at the sinking figure, "Milly, grab hold." The leather cat-o-nine-tails dangled just over her head. "Quick, reach for it," she yelled.

She wasn't even sure if Milly could see it, she looked so confused. Bitsy stretched as far as she could and dangled the leather strap almost to Milly's outreached hand that was clawing at the air. She grabbed at it and missed but then as her head began to disappear again, and the brackish, foul water washed over her, her fingers closed around the knotted end. Most of the sailors stood watching, unable or not interested in helping. They too feared the water. It was a rare sailor who knew how to swim.

A very large black slave appeared from nowhere. His body barely covered by a ragged shirt and too short pants. He grabbed the whip from Bitsy in a strong but badly scarred hand. He leaned over as far as he was able "You hold on girl. I gits you up here."

He was big and he was powerful. "You git me a rope," he said to no one in particular. "G'wan now, find me rope." And within seconds a worn piece appeared. Tying it firmly around his wrist he dangled it down to Milly who had let the slippery leather strap slip from her grasp.

"Grab dat end of the rope an' wrap it 'round yer wrist and we gonna pull you up." His voice was loud. He didn't need to yell.

As fearless as Milly was, her eyes were wide with fright. Hearing the confident words of encouragement, she did as she was told. Deftly, the strong dark arms pulled up the sopping girl, the rope tangled firmly around her wrist.

"There now," he said, "You be fine. Big John save you." Then as quickly as he had appeared, he disappeared back into the crowd.

Bitsy hugged her shivering friend and held her hand tightly, unable to speak. Milly had the look of a stringed marionette, stiff and clumsy, with her mass of red curls firmly matted around her pale face. The terror was etched deep in the depths of her eyes. She ignored the water that ran in rivulets down her arms and legs, leaving a trail. A trail that would soon disappear in the morning sun.

"It's alright, it's alright now," said Bitsy finding her voice. The morning chill made her teeth chatter or perhaps it was the fright. They were ignored and left to their own terrors as they huddled together. The others lost interest in the drama and instead stared in fascination as life unfolded on the docks.

Ships were being loaded or unloaded with all manner of goods. There were bales of cotton and bunched tobacco and what looked like piles of dried fish. A sack fell off the loading platform and broke open. Flour flew through the air bringing curses from the dockworkers. A ship, stinking badly of who knows what, was making its way to the dock. Black faces lined the rails, a deck hand behind them cracked his whip, while yelling curses. Sailors called back and forth to the crew as they tried to tie the newly arrived ship to the dock.

The girls wrinkled up their noses. Indescribable smells from rotting fish and other unnamed garbage and offal that was fouling the streets scented the air around them. But there was also the scent of the morning cook fires that just made their stomachs rumble.

Everyone was busy, rushing back and forth, giving little attention to the new arrivals. Bitsy heard bits of French as men with their neatly tied cravats were descending from carriages driven by African slaves in fine livery. Much like London, street urchins yelled back and forth darting between the disinterested pedestrians. The destitute sat on corners with outstretched arms begging for a coin or piece of bread. She saw few ladies, however. It was the waterfront and not an area where women were commonly seen.

Fishmongers called out their wares, with deep baskets balanced on wide hips. Planks were set up on barrels with farmer's offering eggs. Chickens scratched about, unaware that they would soon be in the cook pot of a Baltimore housewife. Kitchen help from the homes of the local gentry wandered about, stopping first at one merchant then another; their baskets held rounded loaves of fresh bread or vegetables and fruits. They poked at a small piece of blue veined cheese or ran their hands over sausages linked with thick thread. There was bartering back and forth, and some good-natured insults tossed about.

"You call that cheese?" asked one kitchen girl, "I seen better served to the hogs."

"Well then go to their trough and pull some out," yelled the man as he wiped his grimy hands on his apron.

Bitsy's mouth watered looking at all the fresh foods spread about for anyone to purchase. She'd give anything for that hunk of cheese that the kitchen girl refused, saying it was meant for the pigs.

The girls stayed close together. Milly's rag of a dress thinner than the poorest petticoat had dried quickly. Their eyes darted about the crowd. "Look," Milly said almost giggling, "me legs won't hold me. You'd think I'd a-been in the rum."

Bitsy smiled back as she wobbled about with her friend, trying to keep her footing. It had been too many weeks on a ship being endlessly rocked and tossed back and forth; they were unaccustomed to standing and not swaying about with each step. Clinging to each other they made their way across the first solid ground that they'd been on since leaving England so many weeks ago.

The sailor with the ragged eye patch flicked his cat o' nine tails, warning the two hundred odd surviving passengers to stay in line and not stray. They had been warned that to run away meant instant death. The crew would take care of that. It was easy to see that the prisoners all considered servitude the better of the two.

The hawkers and shoppers took no apparent notice of the group as they were led single file to a warehouse that was near falling down from age and neglect.

They never even looked our way, thought Bitsy. How often must this happen? Do ships land daily disembarking human cargo?

The warehouse was dark and smelled of decaying bodies. But the girls breathed a sigh of relief when they were ordered to sit on the hard packed dirt floors; their legs, unaccustomed to walking, were tired and they collapsed in a heap.

The steamy heat in the warehouse became increasingly more oppressive as the day wore on. The sun was high in the sky when two huge

African slaves, their bodies crisscrossed with pink slash marks, rolled in four barrels, all leaking water. The crowd surged forward. Stepping on each other with disregard, their throats parched to soreness, they shoved and pushed to get to the only relief they'd seen in hours.

"Get outa da way," Bitsy was told more than once as she was thrust aside. An old man with flowing gray hair stringy from too much dirt, elbowed his way through and stuck his head deep in the barrel, the water spilling over the rim. Greedy hands pulled him away.

An old woman clawing her way to the front tripped and went down. Feet trampled over her. Bitsy tried to pull her up but the woman only spat at her and told her to leave her be.

Little was left when the two girls succeeded in getting close enough to the barrels. They had to tip one on its side to scoop up the remaining dirty water. It did little to quench their thirst.

Leaning heavily on each other, they half walked, and half crawled back to their corner to rest. The heat continued to rise in the still air. Dozing for a while, they succumbed to the numbing effect of the thick hot air.

Rumbles of thunder growling in the distance woke them. Drowsy still and aching to get more sleep, they jumped when the doors were thrown open.

A fresh breeze entered the stifling room, as the two Negro slaves returned. There was loathing in their eyes as they looked around at the masses of stinking bodies. "Why aren't they sympathetic," said Bitsy, looking at them curiously. "They must know what it's like to lose your freedom."

"Ha," said Milly, "We might be better off than they are, and they know it!"

They scrambled as the slaves pitched a few dozen loaves of bread and some salted fish at them. They let them work out the distribution among themselves, well aware that there wouldn't be enough for all the bodies crammed into the warehouse. Their duty done, they slammed the doors shut, locking them in for who knew how much longer.

Milly, ever quick to seize an opportunity, had scrambled forward but wasn't fast enough. She was able to tear off only one small piece from a loaf before it was ripped out of her hands by a man with claw like hands. He appeared to be blind; one eye squinted up, the other merely an empty socket.

Bitsy had scavenged the floor and had come

up with one very small piece of salted cod. The girls shared the crust of bread and the bit of fish, savoring each bite, careful to not waste a crumb. It had been too long a time since either had tasted bread.

"Me guess would be that was dinner," said Milly, almost wanting to laugh but not sure if she remembered how.

"At home we gave better to Cook's chickens," said Bitsy, as she inspected her hands for just one more crumb, "But I thank you my friend."

"I'm the only friend you've ever had if me memory serves me right."

Bitsy smiled, a tight bitterness twisting one corner of her mouth, as she pushed back the damp curls that stuck to her forehead. "I guess that'd be right. I've never had a friend before. And so, my only friend," she said trying again to smile at the reclining Milly, "now what do we eat?"

"We'll worry about that tomorrow," Milly said, "I do believe we were better off not eating that salted fish."

"Why?" asked Bitsy, "I'd think anything would be better than nothing."

"You watch," said her friend, "and it's not only because I don't favor fish."

And sure enough as the night wore on they could hear more and more curses and groans. One after another of the starving group came close to insanity from the thirst that the salted fish had caused. The girls stayed tight against the splintery wall, trying to stay well out of the way as fights broke out. Even the coolness of the night air did not calm hot tempers.

Morning came but not soon enough for two of the inhabitants of the warehouse. They lay dead on the floor, whether from starvation, bad food or a quarrel with someone was hard to tell. The others gave the two bodies a wide berth; in death their sightless eyes stared into the dim nothingness.

Shafts of sunlight streamed between the ill-fitting boards of the warehouse walls. Sounds from the town seeped in. Bitsy jumped as the doors were thrown open. Two burly men walked in leading a horse drawn farm cart. Water sloshed over the sides from the barrels that were carried on the bed of the cart.

The thirsty mob pushed forward, and the men, muscles taut, shoved them back. "Awright you flea bitten scum of the earth, women and children first. We gonna pour water in these here troughs. We want you up on the back of this here wagon scrubbing yo'selves 'til you 'bout shine."

The larger of the two men spoke, enjoying his temporary authority. "Ya git it right and we gonna' feed ya. Now we gonna' stand right here and see that you do it, and no fightin' or I'm gonna' give you mess of rabble somethin' to fight about." He laughed as he jumped up on the back of the wagon and stood, his arms, bulky with muscle, crossed over his chest. "Get on up here."

The women hesitated only a moment, then moved almost as one to get their fill of drink from one barrel and then to try to wash at the trough. There were bulky cakes of soap to share - yellow with tallow. Bitsy was shoved forward with the first group and was able to get nearly half a cup of water to drink. She moved over to the trough scrubbed at her lice infested hair.

It was impossible to wash their clothes but most splashed water on themselves. Even without clean rinse water, she felt good, almost clean. What was left of her chopped off hair formed a cap of thick, shiny curls. She looked at her hands. Months of grime was still imbedded under and around her ragged fingernails; she wondered if any of it would ever wash away.

"Alright you bunch a' rabble, out. All o' ya',"

bellowed the man acting as the water guard. The water troughs were nearly empty, with only a scum of dirty water at the bottom. The man uncrossed his arms and began to flick his whip, the barbed end producing a few winces as it touched hunched over backs.

Dripping wet with rivulets of dirty water, they let themselves be led out into the morning sunshine. Their eyes first squinting in the bright sunlight, then opened wide in disbelief. They were met by the sights and smells of two overburdened tables that held a bounty of food. More food than most had seen in their entire lives: stacks of cornbread, piles of small loaves of bread and cheese and grapes and dried beef.

"Help yo'selves, you bunch a flea bags, then we'll see what yer really worth. We'll be takin' you over to meet yer new masta's." This was followed by rowdy laughter. The man with the whip took pokes at people as they walked by. "This here food is comp-li-ments of the captain," he said, emphasizing each syllable, "He plans to fatten ye' all up 'fore he gets the money owed fer yer passage."

Milly, not needing a second invitation, grabbed Bitsy's arm, "Be quick," she said as she dragged her around to the other side of one of the long tables. "Quick. Start here. Less apt to be trampled," she said. Grabbing with both hands they gorged themselves, stuffing their mouths with cheese and bread.

"We need to slow down," said Milly, "Eat slowly," she said, her mouth stuffed with bread, crumbs sticking to her chin. "It's sick we'll be if we eat too fast." Bitsy could hardly understand what she said but smiled and stuffed in another piece of slightly stale cheese.

"Aw'right now that be enough. G'wan and sit under those there trees 'til we need ya'." He pointed his whip to the grassy fenced area. He didn't need to call a halt to the banquet that had been set before the starving array of bodies; there was nothing left.

The two girls made their way over to the shade of an oak tree. The others, satiated by the food, sprawled in the grassy area with the morning sun beating down, enjoying the feel of the clean air and the warmth from the sunshine. The girls, comfortable, their stomachs nearly full, drowsed as the morning dragged on.

The sun rose higher in the sky as more people began to crowd under the shade of the oak's spreading branches. The man with the whip began to call them forward, pointing to one, then another; first a young boy, then an older woman, then two small girls who could have been sisters. Then with more than half the people gone, he pointed his whip at Bitsy.

"Get up there," he snarled. "You gonna fetch a pretty penny, young miss. A bit scrawny perhaps but ye' have a healthy look about ya'. Get on up there now, and I'll be warnin' ye'," he said, jerking on her arm, "If ye' open yer mouth and say a word it'll be in the gaol for ye', and we'll leave ye' there 'til the buzzards sup on yer bones. Now keep yer mouth shut and stand up tall. The cap'ain needs to get a good price fer ye' - pay fer yer passage and all."

Bitsy's blue eyes shot sparks of indignation. She wanted very much to pull her arm from his steel grasp, but he stood just behind her; his grimy hand with a vice like grip kept her still.

Slowly, the realization came to her. They were selling her!

This was real. They were selling all the people from the ship to pay for their passage. Call it indenture or whatever they wanted; she was going to go to the highest bidder. That's why they'd had them wash and then fed them that huge quantity of food. She looked over at the remaining group. This was the best they were ever going to look, thanks to their recent care.

Bitsy turned her attention back to the bidding; the gavel fell with a bang, and she was dragged off the stage. She had been sold to someone who would pay her passage across the ocean and then keep her for however many years he bargained for.

She looked back. Where was her friend? She watched a moment as Milly was pushed up to the spot that she'd just vacated. There were no words between them.

"... one of the unhappy Number"
Letter, 1756

"Where am I?" She rubbed at her eyes. It was hard to remember how she'd come to be sleeping on the cold earth. Squinting into the gloom she shook her head and rubbed at the sleep in her eyes. It was a stable to be sure. The unmistakable stench from the unclean stalls made that a certainty. She remembered little of how she'd gotten here. No food since yesterday and a long day in the hot sun in the back of a splintery farm wagon was something she didn't need to recall.

Looking down, Bitsy saw the remnants of what was left of the finely tailored frock that she'd worn that day when she'd ridden out on Destiny. Could it really have been that long ago? A whole season had come and gone since she'd been snatched from her birthplace. Now here she was in this barbaric land with neither kith nor kin.

Even her shipboard friend, her only friend, Milly, had gone a different way. She ran her fingers through her chopped off hair. It had regrown some, long enough to curl behind her ears. It felt a little cleaner than it had for months after yesterday's hasty scrubbing. The curls in this damp and humid climate had turned into a mass of unruly tangles.

Even after her scrubbing she could still feel lice scurrying through the thick mass of short hair and along her scalp. Why bother trying to catch them? Her skin was so infested with vermin it was hardly worth the effort. She scratched first at her foot, then at her leg. Welts and sores from insect bites covered her body. The intense itching never ended. She hadn't had a change of clothes since leaving the estate in England. She couldn't remember when she'd last had a real bath.

"Get up, ya' sleeping cur. What d'ya think this is, a holiday? Get yer lazy bones down to that field now!" The man standing over her lashed out, the barbed end of his whip kicking up a clod of dirt at her bare feet.

"I beg your pardon," she sputtered. She rose and shook out what was left of her ragged dress. She marveled that she was still able to tell that it had once been a deep bottle green. There was still one small piece of gold trim near the waist, which she'd finger every now and again. The hem had been ripped out long ago. Both sleeves had been torn off just above the elbow when they'd become so tattered that they were hanging in shreds. Her once white petticoat was so dirty it was hard to remember it had ever been anything but brown. The entire outfit had been fitted perfectly by the seamstress that her father employed. It was now much too big around and much too short. She looked down at her bare feet.

"Girl, you gonna' daydream all day? You git yo'self out there now or you gonna be feelin' the sting o' my whip." He spit lavishly into the already soiled hay. "I been lookin' everywheres for you. This where you been hidin' out?" he said, more as a statement than a question.

Bitsy hurried to the door, barely looking at the person who had bellowed the orders. She looked out into the misty morning; a fog hung close to the ground blurring the image of the jumbled line of field hands. They were heading down a trail, away from the shacks that must have been their homes.

Where was she and who was this man? She knew better than to question, not wanting to incur his wrath as he flicked his whip. Dazed, confused and not sure what was expected of her, she moved quickly to join the line. The man with the whip was close behind. There were over thirty people, some old, some young; some were hobbling on sore feet or lame legs, most in varying shades of brown, all with eyes down cast. Most she was sure were slaves. It was hard to tell if any were indentures. Where were they going?

Placing one bare foot in front of the other, she slowed her pace as she joined the mass of people. The dust of the path felt soft; only an occasional sharp rock tried to penetrate the bottoms of her feet. Months on the ship with its nearly petrified decks had toughened her soles: they had become as thick and hard as old leather; it was as if she'd always gone barefoot.

It almost made her laugh to remember the five elegant pairs of shoes that she'd left in England. She tried to remember them. There was a pair for every occasion: afternoon tea, practical shoes for her walks in the country with her father, her best leathers for Sunday service, her everyday pair and then of course the riding boots that her father had had the cobbler specially craft for her last birthday. More than once she had regretted taking them off that day when she was at the lake walking Destiny.

Now she was barefoot along with most of the slaves. Why was life playing this cruel joke on her? What was to become of her, she thought, as her stomach growled in hunger? Then, as if he had read her thoughts, there was a crack of the whip and, "Git in that line there, girl or I'll be makin' short work o' you."

She jumped back into the ragged line with the workers and continued to follow, her head held high. Looking around at the hunched shoulders and the lack of interest in anything around them, she caught the eye of one young girl who was staring at her curiously. The girl couldn't have been more than eight or nine, too young for the disfiguring bright pink scar that ran from the corner of her eye down to the corner of her mouth. It gave her a permanent half smile.

Bitsy ignored her turning her attention to the endless fields before them. The overseer, his voice holding a warning, barked orders. Stopping in front of Bitsy, he shoved a heavy hoe into her hands, the sharp blade glinting dully in the morning light. "Here, girl, you go on down them rows and git' them weeds out 'tween them plants."

Questions rose to her lips but froze in place when she looked into the slit like eyes of the person giving the order. He was neither black nor white, but more of a café au lait color, with hateful eyes and unruly black hair that had never seen a pair of scissors; when he spoke, he revealed a row of broken yellowed teeth.

"G'wan, girl, or you'll be feelin' the sting of my whip sure 'nuf."

Bitsy took the tool that he shoved at her and moved in the direction that he pointed. Gripping the unfamiliar smooth handle tightly in her hands, she looked over at the girl with the scar and tried to copy her chopping motion. Striking down hard with the hoe, she was horrified to see the tall green plant fall over.

"Oh dear!" and then even more horrifying was the surprise of feeling a leather strap slashed across her back. She sucked in her breath and bit her lower lip, a surprised grunt escaping as she let the heavy tool fall from her hands. The strap had ripped open both her dress and the flesh beneath; a stinging, searing, white-hot pain burned across her back.

"This just cannot be borne," she thought, as she felt her knees crumple. The cool earth was there to greet her as she fell into a heap. Her eyes fluttered as she struggled to remain conscious but the combination of no food or water, the early hour and then being struck down was too much. She felt the darkness wash over her as she sank into a blessed unconsciousness.

"... that you'd not serve an Animal,"
Letter, 1756

A dark work worn hand with its light tan palm reached out and patted her arm. "It be awright chil', don' you fret none, we gonna' have you back to rights in no time. Here, drink dis stew down, yer gonna' be fine. Now don' go thrashin' about so or yer gonna' tear open that wound."

"Where am I?" Bitsy tried to sit up, leaning on one elbow. Searing pains streaked across her back.

"You be in my cabin. Big Jim bring you by in the wagon an the Mistress done said I be the one to go an' tend to you. She say Massa paid good money fer yo' passage fer indenture and they don' wanna lose ya the first day."

"Big Jim?" said Bitsy.

"Ahyup," she said. "He say he see you awhile back when y'all get off that ship. He say you be wif the one who fell in that water."

Taking a deep breath, she seemed to be un-accustomed to so much talk. With eyes never meeting the young girls, she continued. "Massa dun had a talk wif Louis, that be the overseer that struck you down. Lawd da' Massa was some upset wif him, I tell you."

"Ouch!" cried Bitsy, tears catching on her long dark lashes. She bit her lip, trying to hold back a sob. She hated crybabies and was not going to cry in front of this strange dark woman. "It hurts so," she said.

"I knows that, chile, got a few o' 'em on my back too, more'n I can count I'd say. It be bad fer awhile, but in jus' a few days it be better. We gonna have you good as new. There be a bit o' my green ointment I put on it, that'll help some. Don' smell the best but it gonna' work jus' fine, you see soon enuf."

Bitsy tried to sit up and keep her stinging back from moving. It hurt almost beyond endurance. She had never been struck in her entire fifteen years and could not even imagine one human being striking another so.

The dark woman, sadness etched around her eyes, patted her arm. "Here now, you best drink this stew."

Struggling to sit up she looked at the bowl of fragrant liquid, pieces of unidentified meat floating in a thin brine. Her stomach growled loudly. "I'll need a fork please," she said.

"Chil', you best learn somethin' fast if you gonna stay alive here. First," she said holding up one dark finger, "we all be slaves, might call you somethin' different, but you ain't in no better position then I be. Second, you want a fork, you go git up and find one. And third," she continued, "'there ain't no forks down here in slave quarters that I knows of."

Bitsy sat and thought a moment, then tipped the bowl to her lips and without a by-your-leave gulped the entire contents of the bowl, using her fingers to pick out the bits of carrots and meat.

"Now chil', slo' down some. That may be the only bowl o' stew you gonna see for a while."

"That was so good. I really would like some more."

"Ha! So would we all," she said shaking her head, "So would we all," she muttered.

The stooped woman, aged beyond her years, lifted the grey blanket that covered the opening for a door and disappeared outside.

Bitsy fell back on the straw filled mattress, ignoring the pain, and almost instantly fell into a deep sleep. A tiredness that she'd never experienced before crept into her bones and completely engulfed her and would not let her go.

Noises began to prick at the edges of her sleep. Blinking her eyes, not wanting to wake up, trying to recall where she was and how she'd gotten there, she opened her eyes. Three shiny faces were peering down at her.

"Leave me be," she said, coming out more as a gasp - "Who are you?" The three little ones, too shy to speak, ran for the door suppressing giggles. They disappeared into the falling darkness.

"Girl, found some more stew you was lookin' fo'." Lucy offered her the bowl. Bitsy, her hunger painful, nearly gobbled the entire bowl before even taking a breath or wondering again about a fork. She was hard pressed to remember when she'd last had anything quite so wonderful, but then she could not recall ever being quite so hungry.

Lucy chattered on as Bitsy took her finger and cleaned the inside of the bowl, wiping up every last bite, not wasting so much as a drop.

"I tol' the Mistress you be here, she say that be fine. She think on it and may have you come work in her kitchen 'stead of down in the field. That take some time fo' she can git to it. You is welcome to stay right here but you sees we only got this here room wif only them two mattresses and there be six of us."

Bitsy looked around the tiny one room shack with the hard packed dirt floor and one tiny opening that was supposed to be a window, insects flying in and out at will. It was hard to believe this was someone's home. How could this shelter anyone from the winter winds? There were wide spaces between the boards on the cabin walls, and with the one small fire in the makeshift fireplace there would be little warmth.

"I appreciate the offer. I'm fine. There's room up by the horses," she said easing herself up from the straw filled pallet.

"Lucy, is that your name?" she asked and without waiting for an answer, "Who is this overseer, the man with the whip? He doesn't seem like one of the slaves, but he looks like one of them and everyone is made to listen to him."

"Well now I can tell you this," said Lucy her reluctance slowing her speech. "Some say he somehow be related to the Massa."

"What? How can that be?"

"Don' know. Heard there was some messin' round 'tween Massa and one of them slaves. Heard tell she done had a baby jus' before they sold her off." She stopped suddenly, "don' know any more'n that," she said abruptly.

"I'm not sure what you're telling me," said

Bitsy, "I can't imagine why they'd keep such a horrid man here. He's going to kill someone."

Lucy grunted and chose to ignore the last remark. Bitsy shuffled towards the door; nodded to Lucy and slowly, working out the stiffness, made her way back up the hill.

The sun had sunk below the horizon. Bitsy stood a moment and watched as the last bit of light faded in the western sky. How has this happened, she thought? How has it all come to this? Maybe it's all just a bad dream and I'll wake from it soon. Somehow, she knew that was not going to be how this horror was going to end.

Entering through the small side door of the stable, she wound her way through the carriages and down to where the horses were kept. Looking about, she tried to find a pile of hay that she could turn into her new home. There was a ladder leading up to a hay filled loft, perhaps that would do. Her bare feet took her up the splintery rungs. The horses, settling down for the night, whinnied quietly, as if welcoming her to her new quarters.

"... you do not halfe enough"
Letter, 1756

Bitsy worked hard that first week, trying to blend in, to be just another field hand. She worked especially hard at avoiding the overseer, Louis, and his evil whip. Most mornings she would simply follow the group of workers and try to do whatever they did. Most often it was hoeing, at which she had become quite proficient. With that very first strike of her hoe followed by the snap of the whip, she had learned just what was a tobacco plant and what was a weed.

The hot endless days in the field working with the heavy, long handled hoe left her hands raw and bleeding. Calluses had begun to form around the blisters on her previously smooth white hands. How shocked her family would be, she thought, to see the once fine hands that had played the pianoforte and worked at nothing more taxing than needlepoint and writing out her lessons. They now looked much like the work worn hands of a slave. Lucy had given her a bee's wax salve to put on the broken skin the first night when she had returned from the fields.

"Here ya' go," she'd said, "Made it myself. Made mos' all da medicines round here. Use my herbs jus' like I been taught. I can cure jus' 'bout anything. You go on and try it, you gonna' see," she'd said. And slowly Bitsy did see the healing powers of the salves that Lucy had her spread on all the bad places.

She'd taken to eating her meals with Lucy and her family. They had more than most as Lucy was a "house Nigra" as she called herself and the Mistress tolerated her taking some of the extras back to her shack on slave row. Either the main house had forgotten of Bitsy's existence, or they just let everyone fend for themselves, but no food had ever been sent out to the stable save for the horses' food. The hollow feeling of hunger never left Bitsy's empty stomach.

Dinner at Lucy's usually consisted of corn bread or corn meal mush with an occasional small potato or a bit of rice and then sometimes a ham hock for Lucy to make a stew. Some nights they had no more than a few ears of corn with salt to spread over the kernels. But even then, they considered themselves fortunate, as most slaves had even less to eat.

With the four young ones to feed it was hard to take more than just the most meager portion. When the little they had to eat was done with, Bitsy would head back up the hill to the barn and climb the ladder into the loft, burying herself like a cocoon in the thick hay.

The warmth from the animals kept the barn almost comfortable. She had acquired one moth eaten blanket from the horse's stall, but there was nothing else, not even a rag to wash with or a change of clothes.

Mornings she'd wake early when she heard the first noises of the coming day. She would take time to walk through the end of the building that housed the horses, helping herself to an ear of dried corn from the corncrib. Going down the line of stalls, she'd give each one a pat and call to them by name. "Good morning Beauty, hello Rupert, you're looking fine this morning, and there now Drummer here's some fresh hay."

Usually there were a dozen or more, depending on whether there were houseguests staying at the plantation. She'd hand each a bunch of fresh hay and speak quietly to them. Memories of home would flood over her.

There was a large, skittish gelding that reminded her so much of Destiny back in England, that it made her heart ache. They called him Thunder. He was a glossy chestnut brown with an angular white patch on his forehead much like Destiny's patch. He was just as spirited as Destiny had been. Often, she'd find him nervously prancing about his stall just longing to run.

"Ah, to ride you out over the fields - what fun we'd have," she'd say on her morning visits. Then she'd pat his neck once more before making her way to Lucy's to see if there was anything to eat before heading down to the rows and rows of tobacco that needed to be tended.

During the day, sweating with the heavy hoe clutched tightly in her hands, she'd dream of riding Thunder through the fields to her freedom, imagining what it'd be like to have the wind whistling past her. Often, she imagined that it was his whinnying that she heard as it floated up from the field where they were penned.

"Someday," she whispered, "Someday, you and I will ride together."

It was at the beginning of her second month in the tobacco field that Bitsy found she'd gotten quite good at making herself numb to all the abuse that went on around her. The overseer, free with his beatings, spared no one. His meanness and bitterness oozed from his every pore. She knew to stay as far away from him as she dared.

In the morning when she was given her hoe she'd walk far down the field and start at the end of one of the long rows of the green tobacco plants and hoe back to where the slaves were busy. Louis, cruelty etched forever around his eyes, gave her that liberty, finding that she was fast and worked better by herself. And Bitsy, noticing that the overseer was quicker in the morning to strike out at someone, she knew that was the time to stay the furthest away.

One oppressively hot summer morning, the kind when the cicadas announce the heat of the day before the sun is even fully up, and the once bright green of the summer foliage has a fine covering of dust, and the leaves and trees are perfectly still in the humid air, and the day is so still that if you stood a moment, you would probably hear the munching of caterpillars, Sally became his target. At just ten years old she was Lucy's oldest.

Louis stood next to her, flicking his whip.

He decided she wasn't moving fast enough picking off the tobacco hornworms and squishing them under her bare feet. Sally had a shy but sunny personality. She would hold her head at an angle when she spoke with anyone, trying to conceal the vivid pink scar that ran from her eye to the corner of her mouth. And if she liked you, she'd look you in the eye instead of staring down at her feet.

"So, Sally," he began, while slapping his whip against the side of his threadbare trousers, "what have we here? Are we becoming squeamish maybe? Don' see as yer movin' all that fast this mornin'. Is it my whip you're waitin' for to get you goin'?" Even Bitsy knew he must have been in a vile mood because for whatever reason he usually paid little attention to Sally.

She tried to ignore him and kept on searching for the caterpillars, first under one leaf then the other. Carefully she would pluck each of the fat green pests off and squish it in the soft dirt.

Keeping her eyes down and her head lowered she answered in her soft voice, "Goin' fast as I can, Sir, not many o' dem bugs left."

"Why, Sally, my girl, there's one right there. Have you no eyes?" His whip snapped into the brownish red dirt at her feet, missing her bare toes by inches. The whitish scars on her legs told of other encounters with the strip of leather. Bending, she pulled the green caterpillar off and dumped him into the dirt, squishing him under her heel.

"That's better," he said.

But that was not going to be the end of it. Today she was the one who he'd chosen to harass and torment, and that was exactly what he did for most of the morning. No matter how fast her fingers flew, it failed to satisfy him. He berated and criticized and stood over her yelling and flicking his whip.

At noon when stale bread and warmish water was brought down to the field workers, he flicked his whip one last time before ambling over to the side of the field. Stretching out in the shade of the gnarled old oak, his eyes were soon closed. Sally, along with everyone else gave a sigh of relief. They knew he tired easily in the hot afternoon sun. Most days soon after lunch, he would recline for hours in the shade of the tree.

"Ah relief," sighed Bitsy. "Sally, come sit here while we eat." She made room for her young friend in the shade as they shared their bit of cornbread and lukewarm water. "I wonder if the master has ever seen Louis in that position, napping under the tree," she mused out loud. To be sure, she wasn't going to be the one to interrupt him, for this was the only time when they could talk quietly between themselves, without his telling them to shut their mouths and keep working. And today in the foul mood he was in they were all glad he'd gone off early to take his nap.

Most often after he roused himself from his afternoon siesta, he would begin his cruelty again and then continue on until he decided it was quitting time, and they could all go. More often than not they would work until just before the sun went down. Then he would follow the field workers back to their shacks on slave row, flicking his whip all the way down the path.

On this oppressively hot summer evening, after their long day, and just before the sun had set, there was the rumble of a late day thunderstorm that was gathering strength low on the horizon. Dark clouds churned, and the first few flashes of lightning streaked across the sky. Louis, still in a particularly vicious mood, even after his siesta, had been flicking his whip at the heels of the boys coming out of the fields, telling them to get along. Sally walked next to Bitsy; both kept their heads down and said nothing, trying to become invisible while the overseer walked along behind them. Sally, in her tiredness, tripped, falling to her knees.

"C'mon Sally, get yerself up, you lazy no account. You can walk." He flicked his whip into the dust just inches behind her feet. "C'mon, there's nothing wrong with you, girl. Get up."

Sally, tiredness all over her, appeared to sink deeper into the soft dust. The light had gone out of her eyes. Bitsy leaned over to help her up as the whip sang through the air. It landed solidly on Sally's back.

"That'll learn ya'," he said, a menacing grin pulled tight across his face. The crack and the moan that came from her lips sparked something inside of Bitsy. Something deep down and as yet unknown. With no thought as to what she was doing, she spun around and grabbed the leather strap. Yanking it with a strength she didn't know she had, she tried to rip it out of his hand.

Startled to speechlessness, he pulled it back from her, ripping open her flesh, then quick as a flash cracked it in the air and brought a lash down on the infuriated girl's back. It ripped wide what was left of her tattered dress and split the skin open on her recently healed back.

Facing him, tears stinging her eyes from the pain, she spat out at him, "How dare you," her eyes seething with hatred. "Just who do you think you are? How dare you strike me. You will never do that again I can promise you."

Louis, his face frozen in a horrible grin, eyed Bitsy, hardly believing that a mere field hand would defy him so. He raised his whip, murder in his eyes, intending to strike her down once and for all. Bitsy was quick.

She turned on her heel and sprinted off the path, into the long grass in the field, her tattered skirt held high with one hand, her bare feet hardly touching the ground, knowing her life depended on getting as far away from him as she could.

Her only chance she knew would be to outrun him. Her feet fairly flew over the dried grass. She would not be caught; she would not let that brute of a man ever touch her again. The split rail fence loomed before her just as the tip of his whip, like a stinging wasp, touched the small of her back. His heavy breathing was close behind her. Knowing he wouldn't attempt to follow her into the horse's pen she scrambled over the wooden rails. Catching her dress on the splinters, she ripped it free. He wouldn't follow; he hated horses, nearly as much as they hated him. Thunder was standing at the water trough, head up, ears alert, looking over at what all the commotion was about.

Bitsy caught her breath, gnawing on her lower lip. Her steps made no sound. "Thunder, it's me. Come, Thunder," she spoke as calmly as she was able, sweat and blood pouring down her back, the sting of it nearly bringing her to her knees. "Come Thunder, it's only me."

She held out her trembling hand as though bearing a gift. Thunder eyed her, not quite trusting. Approaching cautiously, she continued murmuring quiet words to him, then reached out her hand and put it on his warm coat. Putting one foot on the water trough and grabbing a handful of his long mane she swung her leg up over his back. Digging her heels into his sides she shrieked, "Go Thunder, go boy."

Thunder needed little urging. He moved with the speed of a flash of lightning. He knew where the low point was in the fence and that was the direction he chose. Tucking his legs up close to his body, he easily cleared the top rail. Galloping towards his freedom he was barely aware of his small charge clinging for her life on his back.

White knuckles showing, she hung on, eyes closed tightly; rider and horse moved as one. The wind whooshed by. The heavens had held off long enough; they opened up and the rain from the gathering storm let loose with earsplitting fury, both stinging and then soothing the ripped flesh on her back. She was soaked. It had taken only moments.

The lightning cracked and flashed and streaked across the sky, the thunder crashed and banged and rumbled to a deafening pitch; each new clap shook her to her very bones. The horse kept up at full speed, maybe from the frightening sound of the wildness of the summer storm or maybe from the joy of being set free. His pace slowed only when his sides were heaving to the point of bursting.

The dark had closed in; the warm rain was slowing to a sprinkle. The storm had worn itself out and was very nearly over. The horse, making his own way, found a path to follow through a thicket and then along the edge of the woods. Bitsy was losing strength as the animal, exhausted from his run to freedom, slowed to a walk. Her grasp loosened on the horse's thick mane; she was barely able to keep her balance on his steaming back.

As the moon came out from behind the last of the thick, dark clouds, she could no longer hold on. Her grip loosened and the horse's burden slipped to the ground. She landed in a heap at the side of the wooded trail, her cropped curls shining dully in the pale-yellow moonlight, her breathing slowed to almost nothingness. The darkness surrounded her like a protective blanket.

"*my sufferings here . . .*"
Letter, 1756

Tucked into the thicket by the side of the road, damp with the morning dew, Bitsy rubbed at her eyes, trying to remember where she was and what had happened. For a moment she lay still staring up as grey clouds drifted lazily across the sky. The light from the early morning sun was just beginning to brighten the greyness of the overcast day.

The sound of a horse and the creaking wheels of a farm wagon brought her back to her plight. She tried to rise but found she could not. The slash across her back was so painful she could not lean on her arm to get up and gain her footing.

The wagon was fast approaching. She need-ed to hide. But where? The horse was gone. How could she escape? The penalty for running away as an indentured servant was stiff. Too late, she gained her footing. Every bone creaked and ob-jected. The driver of the farm wagon easily saw her; he was nearly within arm's reach.

"What have we here?" He pulled on the reins of the two big farm animals, "'Peers you've had quite a night here at the side of the road. Would you be wanting a ride perhaps?"

Bitsy looked at the well-worn whip on the seat beside the overseer. For a fleeting moment she thought perhaps death would be better than to get into that wagon. Those all too familiar slit eyes that slashed across that dark face bored right through her.

"C'mon now girl, I'll carry ya home." The muscles in his gaunt face pulled back his lips to form a cruel and unnatural smile. It revealed the familiar row of broken yellowed teeth. Louis grasped his whip and slowly and methodically began to slap it against his palm.

Bitsy, loathing each step, limped stiffly over to the rickety farm wagon. She held her head high, staring at him with bold defiance. I will not give in, and I will not give up, she said over and over in her mind. And then - giving it no thought at all, she spat out "I'm not going; you'll have to kill me." She turned on her heel and ran.

He moved like lightning, jumping down from his high seat on the wagon. In less than three strides he had grabbed her by the hair.

"I've heard enough of your sass, girl." In an instant he had a piece of twine wound tightly around her thin wrists. He dragged her back to the wagon. Tying the rope to the wheel he spat and said, "You'll learn to hold yer tongue and do as yer told."

Ready to snap the whip, the sound of a carriage stopped him midway to delivering the first blow. Two matched geldings came up out of the mist pulling a carriage, a carriage that had seen better days. As it pulled up next to them a face appeared at the door.

"Any trouble here?" asked a very ancient and gnarled old man.

Louis did not like being questioned "No sir," he answered. "Just dealing with one of our young boys who can't behave." He tipped his hat to the old man and said, "We're fine, you can be on your way."

"What'd you say," he nearly yelled, cupping a hand to his ear.

"We're fine," said Louis, raising his voice.

"Are you sure now that you don't need some assistance?" he inquired. His voice had the pitch of one who's hard of hearing. He leaned further out of his carriage as he pushed the pince-nez further up the bridge of his nose. Bitsy turned to look not sure if she should cry out but the old fellow was not only near deaf, but his eyes were squinting, trying to bring things into focus.

"Well then here," he said, his voice loud and slightly annoying, "take this poster. Apparently, there's an escaped slave or some such that they're on a search for. You'd best be careful," he warned.

Louis took the paper. "Thank you then," he was close to yelling. He folded the paper and tucked it firmly into the leather pouch that held his tobacco. "We're fine," he said, his voice loud and clear. "You can be on your way." He was loath to admit that like most slaves he wasn't able to read. It wasn't allowed.

The man withdrew into the carriage and banged on the roof letting the driver know they could be on their way. The driver gave them a curious look then turned away, ignoring the two by the side of the road. He flicked his whip and urged the horses forward.

Louis spat into the dirt. He let out a string of curse words and then picked up Bitsy like a sack of moldy cotton and threw her in the back of the wagon. "You were saved that time," he said, "but it won't happen again."

He hopped up onto his seat and flicked the

reins. Bitsy could still hear the carriage and hoped that they'd get closer and then maybe she could loosen her ties and slip off the wagon.

"We're headin' on down to the James Plantation to pick up more Nigras," she heard him say. It was through the fog that was clouding her head. "Ya may not have known that having been gone for a day. We'll be needin' all the help we can git to start pickin' that tobaccy." Then he laughed. Why, she had no idea. Curling up in the corner of the wagon she listened hoping the carriage would get closer, but it turned off at the next crossroad.

Louis talked, rambling on and on for the next few miles. His senseless chatter didn't end until they'd pulled up to the barn of the plantation. A stable boy ran out to hold the horses. Louis jumped down from his seat. He inquired after Micah and said he was there to pick up the goods and buy an indenture. Bitsy bit back a scream, why don't they sell her or trade her. But she knew better than to cry out.

"Hey there, Micah," he said to the approaching man. "Here to pick up them young bucks you'll be lendin' us."

"Well, there they are," he said as he scratched at his unshaven chin. He pointed to a small group of slaves taking their ease under a tree. "Get on over here," he yelled at them.

They appeared to not have heard. With little interest in what was taking place they eased themselves up from the coolness of the shade.

"Get on up in that wagon." he said, giving a shove to the shortest one. He couldn't have been much more than a child.

There was no argument as they climbed up into the back of the creaky wagon. Bitsy with great effort, moved to a sitting position on the bed of the wagon. She wrapped her arms around her legs and rested her forehead on her knees, hoping she'd disappear. They gave her no notice.

"Hey there Louis, who you got back there with that yeller hair?"

"Ha," he answered, "That's the best little indenture we got."

Micah wasted no time making an offer to trade a graying old slave for the young white girl. "She works like any ten Nigras once you put a hoe in her hands," said Louis, "We won't be tradin' this one, no, not yet. She's still got some life in her." He wiped the back of his grimy hand across his mouth, "Say where be that house girl the Mistress asked y'all about?"

"She comin'," said Micah. As he spoke the

words they saw a young girl, with dark auburn curls that were escaping from under her cap, making her way down the path. She had a clean white apron tied primly around her waist. Her bare feet made no sound as she approached the wagon.

"Awright then, let's get her up here. Here's the envelope the Masta' sent, and our business be done. I thank you kindly, Micah. See you in a few days."

The auburn-haired girl lifted her long skirt and climbed up on the wagon, sitting on the tailgate, her legs dangled, nearly touching the ground. Bitsy stole a shy peek, trying not to move any more than necessary. There were eight dark slaves, all different sizes but all with the same tired look of resignation and maybe frustration or anger? She wasn't sure, maybe it was defiance but whatever it was, it wasn't a look that she saw when the owners were there. She wanted to close her eyes and go to sleep but wanted to see who it was at the back of the wagon.

Her eyes widened. Could it be?

Yes! It was Milly.

She gasped and quickly regretted it. She didn't want to be discovered. Ducking her head, she tried to stay hidden behind the hunched over slave sitting next to her, afraid that Milly would cry out if she recognized her.

If Louis knew that they were friends, he would do everything possible to make their lives miserable. And, by the look of Milly she knew nothing about the sting of a whip or the lack of food that was all too common on the Wickerson Plantation. And now she certainly didn't need any trouble brought down on her head the first day with her new employer.

Riding along in silence through most of the morning, the sun beat down, scorching their backs and uncovered heads. The stinging pain from the slash mark on her back made her want to cry out, but instead she only moaned softly as she drifted in and out of sleep swaying with the wagon.

It was an endless ride. They arrived back at their own plantation late in the afternoon. Louis gave orders for Milly to go to the house, "and the rest of you no accounts get yerselves over to that there field." Louis' reputation for cruelty put wings on their feet as they made their way down to the tobacco. There were still enough hours in the day to work the fields.

Bitsy had stayed out of sight of Milly. To

anyone who didn't know her she looked like just another shabbily dressed field hand who happened to be white instead of the dark-skinned slave. Bitsy would get to talk to her friend soon enough, but for now she needed to make her way down to the field with the others.

It had been close to sunset. The hours worked that day were the longest that Bitsy could remember. The back breaking task of slashing the plants and stacking them was so tiring and strenuous, and with the fresh wound on her back stinging from the sweat pouring into it, and her stomach rumbling for lack of food, she knew she wasn't going to make it.

It wasn't long after sunset, as the blackness of the night crept in all around them, while Louis was busy flicking his whip at the borrowed help, that Bitsy once again fell into a crumpled heap between the rows of the thick green tobacco leaves. Louis, scowling his displeasure, walked over. In a dazed fog she could hear him slapping his whip against the palm of his hand. Why doesn't he just end it once and for all, she thought.

It was well known in the slave quarters that he'd been warned by the master that too many of his slaves were being laid up by injuries inflicted by the overseer. The master said he wanted it stopped. Louis however was comfortable with his methods; the master exercised little control over him and rarely interfered. He took the warning lightly. She tried to rise. Louis flicked his whip once more and then mumbled, "Ain't even worth the trouble."

"Big Jim," he yelled, "Get her outta here. Take her to yer woman. She ain't doin' us a lick a good here."

Big Jim bent over and scooped her up, while murmuring unintelligible words. He carried her to the wagon and laid her with an unexpected gentleness on her side so's not to aggravate her back further.

"Lucy ain't gonna be happy 'bout this," he mumbled. He hopped up onto the wagon. "Gid'yup Grady, let's git dis girl to home." He slapped the old mare's back with the worn leather reins.

The cool darkness of Lucy's cabin welcomed her again. Big Jim laid her on the straw pallet and went in search of the healer. It wasn't long before the grey blanket that served as a door lifted and in she walked, a small basket of herbs in hand.

"You sure is one for punishment, now ain't you." With a quiet gentleness she washed and cleaned the raw wound on Bitsy's back, while unintelligible words were mumbled into the darkness. With a practiced touch, she smeared on the sweet-smelling salve. Bitsy bit down on her lip trying not to gasp from the pain.

"Here now chile, put this on," she said, while shaking out a faded gingham dress. "Ain't much left of yours. This be from da' Mistress. She done give it to my Sally, but it be far too big for her yet. You go on and take it." She let out a great sigh. "Mistress say she gonna have Louis hung if he done touch one more of her people. She say soon as Massa return Louis gonna go down the river, she don' care who he be."

Tiredness was in her voice and etched around her eyes. "He costin' them too much money what wif one or 'nother of them field hands always laid up. Now you jus' rest yo'self. You gonna be fine. You ain't the kind to give up. Ol' Lucy gonna make you as right as rain." She helped the young girl into the slightly used cotton shift.

Bitsy stayed curled up on the straw mattress listening to Lucy as she put together the evening meal. The mistress had been particularly generous with her this week and had given her extra leftovers from the big house. As meager as they were, they all knew it was by far better than what most slave households were allotted.

Lucy was a good worker, and hardworking house slaves were hard to find, especially so far north in slave country. Lucy knew what she was doing by serving her Mistress tirelessly and well. She had told Bitsy, "Seems to me dat too many families ha' been broke up when da Massa decides to sell one or more people of our families. So, da' way I sees it, 'long as I be her best house Nigra and she be happy, she won' be sellin' any of my babies."

Oh, just let that be true, thought Bitsy.

Dinner in Lucy's cabin was always late. She'd wait until the main house was served and then bring what leftovers she could down to the family. Tonight, they were more than fortunate to have cornbread, boiled greens, a slice of ham and sweet potatoes. A real treat indeed.

Bitsy, hungry as she was, tried hard to be satisfied with her portion. Lucy had more than most but with Sally and the three always hungry boys it seemed that no matter how much they were served it was never enough.

Lucy proudly passed fragrant rolls nestled in the bottom of a basket lined with a red napkin. When it came to Bitsy, she took her one allotted roll. Tired as she was, she tried to be grateful and pleasant "...And Lucy, isn't this your favorite color? It's all tattered but would work well in one of your quilts."

"Ahhh," she said, "Red been my color since I was a babe. Don' see too much of it. This be da Massa's napkin and they count everythin'. Best I return it from whar it came."

"Too bad," said Bitsy, "It'd look awfully pretty in that quilt for Sally that you've been working on."

"Time enough to finish 'dat one," she replied.

The three boys were already snuggling down into the mattress. "I can help," said Bitsy.

"No need," said Lucy, "I wait for Big Jim to come home."

She needed to be on her way. Biting her lip so's not to cry out, she rose from the floor where she'd been sitting, the pain from the slash a reminder of her earlier encounter.

Bidding them a hushed goodnight, she pushed aside the gray tattered blanket and stepped out into the darkness.

Slowly, the stiffness taking hold, she made her way to the barn. With no light except that from the soft glow of the moon she trusted her memory to find her way.

Pushing the old wood door open, she was greeted by the gentle whinnying of some of the horses. With silent steps she walked down the middle of the hay strewn path to Thunder's stall. There he was, bigger than life, no worse for wear from their unsuccessful escape to freedom.

"Hello, Thunder, my friend, I knew you'd make it back." She opened his stall door and slipped in. Patting his silky forehead, she held out a handful of fresh straw. "There you go boy, you're a good friend. Just think, we almost made it to freedom." She stroked his long powerful neck.

"Who's there?" A voice boomed out of the blackness of the night. "You girl, what're you doing with Thunder? That's my horse. Get out of there."

She stopped; the hair on her neck stood on end. Who was there? The door to the stall opened and she held her breath. Holding his lantern high, she could just make out Herbert Wickerson. She knew who he was. As the son of the master, his reputation as spoiled and pampered and mean, was known throughout the slave quarters although most had never seen him. Where had he come from?

"What are you doing with that horse? You don't belong in here. Who are you?" He held the lantern higher to get a better look.

"I'm Bitsy Sir. I work here on the plantation." She'd heard of this young man's cruelty and knew better than to tell him that this was her home, where she slept and lived.

"I've heard of you. You're the white girl who stole Thunder."

Bitsy tried to edge around to the door to the stall, planning her escape. His bulky body blocked the way, his eyes, reflecting the lantern light, flashed a cold and frightening anger. Maybe she had a chance of ducking past him and out the door and into the darkness.

One hand held the lantern and in the other he had a smoldering pipe. The odor of burning tobacco filled the stall. As he came closer, she could smell the stench of whiskey on his breath. Backing away, she stayed out of arm's reach when Thunder, upset by the burning smell, snorted, and stamped his feet. Herbert was momentarily distracted. Bitsy, quick as a flash, turned to run. His heavy boot missed her by inches as he kicked out at her. The kick he had planned to land on her backside was too late, she had vanished into the darkness.

"...rap ourselves up in a Blanket"
Letter, 1756

It healed, but the wound was a never-ending reminder of the turn her life had taken. The stiffness started to ease. The tiredness, however, and the deep gnawing hunger felt as if it would be part of her forever.

The slaves whispered among themselves that Louis must have been warned – the crack of his whip now rarely met flesh. He preferred to scare them by cracking it over their heads or at their feet, laughing his cynical laugh as he watched them jump and hop to stay out of harm's way.

It was nearing the end of the harvest season but there was still more than enough to do. The nights were becoming chilly, with a hint of frost in the air heralding the approach of winter. Bitsy wore only the cotton dress that Lucy had given her when her green serge riding dress had finally fallen to shreds. She recognized pieces of her old dress in the quilt that Lucy had been making. It reminded her of a former life, one that was so far out of reach that she wondered if maybe she had dreamed it. Had life in the rolling countryside of England been nothing more than a dream?

Lucy's quilt was a medley of scraps of fabric that she collected; she didn't care from what source. Most pieces were from old clothes that were just short of rags or from the bits and pieces left when the seamstress finished with a new frock for the Mistress.

She had two quilts completed for her children and was now working on a third, this one for Sally. It was a riot of color. Each bit of fabric sewn in had a story to tell. When she sat at the fire at night doing her stitching, piecing the salvaged pieces of cloth, she would often chat about bits of her life. She'd tell Bitsy curious fragments, like that she'd been told that she was born on this plantation. She never mentioned her mother other than she too had been a slave. Who her pap was had never been revealed. Perhaps she didn't know.

There was a bit of very faded blue flannel that she had been busy working on. Lucy said it had been from a piece of clothing that Big Jim wore when he first arrived. Sold at auction, she said, from way down in the south. He thought he'd been about 12 years old. He remembered little of his family or chose not to talk about it, whichever, Lucy never probed him too deeply. All he had of his young years was a hand-sewn shirt, long outgrown, but now the pieces would be sewn into the great medley of silent stories.

"And do you know where each scrap came from?" asked Bitsy.

"Most," she answered. "They's lotsa stories here to be told," she said, "Lotsa memories stitchin' it up. It brings it all together. Kinda like life." She guided her needle through the soft fabric. "Got some bright scraps here, bring up warm memories. There be some need a stitch or two to hold 'em together, and some almost too thick to be pierced by a needle." She stopped a moment to smooth the wrinkles. "Some easily fit in," she said, "some colors clash. Some faded that only stand out when there be pieces around 'em. Then some ain't goin' to fit into the pattern no matter where they's placed. And then," she added, more as a mumble than wanting to be heard, "try as you might, no matter how strong the stitches, some just ain't gonna to stay put."

The few bits of the vivid reds stood out sharply against most of the muted squares of the other fabrics. "Red be my color," said Lucy, smiling almost shyly. "Always been my favorite. Jim know that. The day we jumped the broom he surprise me wif' a red bandanna, 'bout wore that thing out. Here it be right over here," she said pointing, "Got a few pieces out of that."

"I see," said Bitsy, admiring the intricate pattern and tiny stitches that were a marvel. "Don't know how you can even see to sew in this light," said Bitsy.

"Oh, I can see well enuf'. Fingers do mos' of the work, don' have to see real well to know which parts go together."

"Pretty colors," said Bitsy enjoying the colorful medley in their otherwise brown and gray world. "Too bad there aren't more of your reds."

"Hard to find," said Lucy and left it at that. Her magic with a needle was legendary. Even the Mistress had recognized her talent but with so many other tasks assigned to her, there was hardly time for the pursuit of her seamstress skills. And now she had been instructed by the Mistress to teach the new house girl, Milly, all about stitching, but there had been little time on such a busy plantation.

Bitsy and Milly had seen each other alone only once since Milly had arrived to become the new house girl. They met when they both had gone to the well early one morning; Milly to get water for the house and Bitsy to fetch water for the horses.

It was a hurried conversation. Milly was almost giggly with joy at discovering Bitsy at the same plantation. She told Bitsy that she now worked for the Mistress as the cleaning girl. Rarely was she allowed out.

"I try to stay out of the way and hidden because of Herbert, the owner's son," she had told Bitsy. "He will not leave me be, he pesters me whenever he's about. There's going to be trouble for sure," she said, "and I'll be puttin' that off as long as possible."

Bitsy hugged her friend, trusting that they weren't being observed. "Oh Milly if we could just get away from here. I don't know what to do. But let me tell you, Herbert couldn't hold a candle to Louis for just plain meanness. You need to avoid him too."

"Bitsy, I've hidden from him more than once. But you too. Be careful. Stay far away from him. I heard tell in the main house that there be some relation to the Master and that be why they keep him on."

"Indeed." She nodded in agreement, "I've heard that, and I imagine it's true. Why else would they have him here?"

"Well, 'tis said in the big house," began Milly looking around to be sure that they weren't being observed, "that when the Master was young, he had befriended one of the slave women and Louis was the result, if you get my meaning." She gave her friend a wink.

"So I've heard, answered Bitsy, a knowing look passing between them. "Can it really be true?"

"Well, 'tis said the Master took a real liking to a young Nigra named Ladygirl, Louis' mother, but she was sold down the river. Louis was real young when that happened, and they say he's been just plain ol' mean ever since." She lifted the bucket off the hook, spilling some of the water and continued in a whisper. "It's said that the master thought the family owed him something, so they've kept him on 'cause they didna' know what else to do with him."

Bitsy wasn't sure if she'd heard correctly. "Good heavens if that's true he's the master's son and Herbert's his half-brother. Milly, that's dreadful." They looked at each other. "Oh my," said one, her hand covering her mouth, trying to suppress a giggle.

"Well, 'tis also said that Lucy came about

the same way but who's to know. Bitsy, quick," she said, "someone's coming." She grabbed her bucket and turned back up the hill to the main house, her head down, her bare feet moving swiftly through the tall grass.

Bitsy, her head down, turned in the direction of the stables, careful not to slosh any water. Was it true she wondered? Did the entire slave quarter know about the relationship? She would have liked to ask Lucy if it was a fact, but she was sure she'd already told her as much as she intended to.

The days wore on. The two continued to watch for a chance meeting. With the endless chores on a busy plantation, it was near impossible. They were unable to meet again.

The nights were longer with the passing days of fall, and the work seemed to never end.

After yet another day of endless hours in the tobacco barn, Bitsy dragged herself away from eating a few ears of corn at Lucy's. Wanting to enjoy the peacefulness of the night, it wasn't to be.

The frigid air had put wings on her feet as she made her way through the cold to her make-shift home in the barn. Winter was fast coming on; icy rain had left sparkling little droplets of mist in her golden curls and soaked her thin cotton frock.

She clomped up the hill in the well-worn, too big leather boots. A gift from Lucy. They were from the main house. They had once been Herbert's, she'd said. They were scuffed and the leather was split at the toe, but they offered some protection from the freezing cold. The noise they made from flip flopping on her feet announced her coming wherever she went. She didn't care. They kept her feet almost warm on cold nights, and usually dry.

It was a pitch-black night, overcast with heavy rain clouds scurrying across the sky. She'd walked this path so many times before she didn't need a light to find her way. So far as she knew, no one in the main house had ever given a thought to where she lived or slept, and she preferred it that way. No one cared what she did as long as she was in line with the rest of the field hands every morning.

Tonight, there was a storm in the air, the wind whipped sharply around the buildings that loomed like ghosts in the dark. She couldn't wait to get up to her hay loft and curl up in the tattered old horse blanket. The blanket was itchy, and flea infested but she had claimed it after it had been carelessly tossed aside and was glad to have it.

Slipping soundlessly through the door, more tired than usual, hungry as always, she shivered from the dampness. Walking by Thunder's stall, she didn't stop for her usual evening greeting, but clip clopped in her too big boots straight to the ladder, her teeth chattering. She had visions of curling up in the scrap of blanket and snuggling down into the straw where she'd be almost warm for the night.

The cavernous barn was enclosed in blackness. There was an unusual, eerie silence; even the horses were mysteriously still. Hardly noticing, she reached the ladder; tiredness overwhelmed her. Her foot rested on the bottom rung. Something shot out from the blackness. It grabbed her arm. Hot fingers bit into her flesh. If it hadn't been such a strong grip holding her up, she was sure she would've fallen over from sheer terror.

"What are you doing here?" hissed a voice out of the darkness. The words were slurred. The stink of whiskey made her gag.

In her tiredness she had failed to notice the glow of a pipe and the smell of tobacco smoke when she had entered. The hand gripping her arm was hurting her.

Thinking quickly and trying to keep the tremor out of her voice, she answered, "Sir, I'm here only to feed the horses."

"You're lying. You're planning on running away again. You and your kind can't be trusted for a minute. Why my father keeps you people here on his plantation is beyond anything I can imagine."

"Sir, I must get to the horses if you'll let me go."

"I'll not let you go. You come over here to me and we'll have some fun."

Bitsy jerked her arm out of his grasp. He struck out at her with one well aimed kick. It landed squarely on her backside, nearly crashing her to the ground. Stumbling, she ran the length of the building, her boots clip clopped, cutting through the deadened silence. She ducked and tried to hide between the carriages, all polished and shiny and ready for the next unknown journey. Now in the darkness they appeared to be monstrous forms looming up out of the shadows, wanting to take possession of anyone who passed.

He was following close behind. There was

nowhere to hide. Stumbling along the splintery wall she felt for the side door. She threw all her weight against it. It flew open. She was back out in the blackness of the night. Slipping out of the boots she took them up and ran.

The darkness and the wind and the icy mist quickly enveloped her. With feet numb from the cold, she slowed to a walk, her feet nearly silent through the icy blades of grass. Moving in the direction of the slave quarters she knew there was a wagon there filled with hay. That's where she could hide. He'd never look there.

Afraid to bring trouble on Lucy's household, she walked far around the slave shacks. The hay wagon had been left at the bottom of slave row. Reaching it, she listened for a moment; knowing he wasn't going to follow, it was too wet and icy and cold, and he'd had too much of his father's whiskey. His father knew nothing of his nighttime drinking and smoking, she was sure of that. If he did know, he most assuredly would not have allowed such an indulgence in one so young.

Pulling herself up over the side of the wagon she burrowed deeply into the hay, grateful for the warmth it offered, out of the freezing cold and sleet. She was going to have to be more careful when returning at night to her secret sleeping place in the loft.

The dark deepened, the clouds thickened, and the icy rain continued to drizzle down. "Don't cry," she whispered to herself, but a sob escaped as she curled up into a tight ball in the hay letting sleep overcome her.

"only this comfort..."
Letter, 1756

Milly had been there waiting for her. Bitsy's heart nearly stopped when she appeared at the ladder to the loft standing in the darkness. It hadn't been that many days since Herbert Wickerson had stood at that exact spot.

It was very late. She had stayed too long, chatting with Lucy. The moonlight had guided her way. Having learned her lesson, caution directed her every step as she entered the barn; she clutched her boots in her hand.

The nocturnal visits to Thunder to bestow one more handful of hay had stopped. She feared for her safety with the owner's son prowling about in the dark shadows. The soreness from the kick he had inflicted on her kept the memory fresh. She would use extra caution to never be caught alone again.

Standing for a bit, she listened to the gentle calls of the horses and the now and again stomping of one of the wakeful animals. Sniffing the air for a trace of tobacco smoke and getting only the warm odor of the animals and their dander she approached her ladder. Keeping a cautious eye to the left and to the right, she peered into the darkness looking for even a trace of light.

Reaching out a hand for the familiar rough rungs of the ladder, a whisper came from the shadows. She nearly swooned from fright. Her heart skipped a few beats. It was her friend.

"What are you doing, Milly, are you mad?" Her voice was just above a whisper. "Don't you know it's not safe? The master's son has taken to wandering about in here."

"Bitsy, could you not help me now? I've run away." Milly's voice cut like a frightened hiss through the darkness.

"You are mad. You can't run away. Where will you run to? There's nowhere to go," she whispered into the blackness. "I tried to run away, and I had nowhere and no one to go to."

"You can help me, Bitsy. I need to hide," her voice just above a whisper, both tense and tired. "Just for a few days, then they'll be calling off the search and I'll be safe. They're all packing for England, and they'll be going in a week, and I don't think they'd be putting their trip off just because a servant girl went and run off."

"Milly, you're mad. I'm so glad to see you, but you truly are mad. You'll be flogged to within an inch of your life. You've got to go back before they miss you."

"Nay, I'll never go back. That lunatic son of theirs kicks me and torments me so's I can't bear it another day." A sob caught in her throat. "Tonight, his father's out somewhere and that son of a seacock kicked me so bad I crashed down the stairs. I nearly couldn't stand back up."

She stopped a moment and wiped at her eyes with the sleeve of her dress. "Lucy heard all the clatter and came and helped me to the kitchen. I hid 'til dark, then made me way here." She whispered the words into the darkness. "No one will even be knowin' I'm not there and they probably won't be missin' me 'til morning." She hiccupped. "Lucy, good girl that she is, splinted and bound up me leg so's I could at least hobble. She says it's broke for sure. Now what am I gonna' do?"

"Milly," she whispered into the darkness, "I don't know what to do. Where can you go?" She reached out and hugged her friend. "Here, I'll help you up the ladder. We'll talk up there."

Bitsy pushed and shoved and half carried Milly up the ladder to her home in the straw.

She gasped whenever any weight was put on her leg.

The dampness of the late fall night had penetrated the girls light cotton shifts. As they shivered together, they shared as best they could the scrap of blanket that Bitsy had found. They snuggled deeply into the straw where they were going to do a full night of talking and planning. Within minutes, however, before they'd hardly uttered a word, both fell into an exhausted and deep sleep.

"Wake up, Milly. It's morning. Wake up." There was no mistaking the distant cock's crow welcoming the dawn.

"Ohhh, I can't," she groaned, "I don't want to wake up. I'm tired and me leg. I can't move me leg. It hurts so, Bitsy. I think it's broke for sure."

"Milly what are we going to do? I've got to go. They'll miss me and know I'm with you. I've got to go now, or they'll come and find us." She struggled out of her warm nest in the hay. "I'll think of something. You stay here."

"And where is it you think I'd be going with this leg? Back to Ireland maybe?"

"Oh Milly, I'm so sorry. I'll think of something. I'll be back." Running her fingers through her hair, pulling out most of the hay sticking in it, she crawled over to the ladder.

"Morning, Thunder," she whispered as she rushed past his stall, not daring to stop. When she appeared at Lucy's hoping to find something to eat, she tried to talk with her alone but Lucy, perhaps knowing of the trouble brewing, said little other than the usual, "Der be some corn, eat up now. I be on my way."

Bitsy stared a moment at the ear of dried corn. The horses ate better. She took a bit of salt and rubbed it on the shriveled yellow ear and thought for a moment that she couldn't eat it. Her stomach was going to rebel, and she'd starve to death. Maybe that would be a better fate. Then she thought of Milly up in the loft with nothing. She sank her teeth into the hard kernels. She was late, they'd miss her and there'd be more trouble. Lifting the grey blanket, she let herself out, all the while munching on the corn.

The day seemed endless. All she wanted to do was to get back to Milly but there wasn't a way that she could slip off. She knew Louis would be suspicious if she suddenly took ill and had to leave.

There was no talk in the fields about the missing servant. It would not be discussed, maybe fearing that they'd be overheard, or maybe they didn't yet know about it. But that was doubtful as they knew and shared most everything, however that was only among themselves. Instead, their melodious tunes floated through the air. Words most times indistinguishable as they used their own language. She was quite sure it was their way to communicate privately.

Bitsy thought it highly unlikely that they didn't all know far more than she did. The grapevine in the slave colony was the most effective sharing of news that she'd ever known. What was said between them however was for their information only and never shared outside of their close group.

The day passed in slow motion. It felt as though it would never end. The sun was dropping below the horizon when they were relieved of their duties. Exhaustion nearly overtook her as she made her way to Lucy's cabin. Hunger gnawed at her empty stomach, but she ate little. Excusing herself early, she told Lucy that she wasn't feeling well and had to leave. The look in Lucy's eyes told her she knew what she was up to.

"Here now," she said, "you take this left-over bread an' this last ear o' corn case you git hungry in the night." It was a great sacrifice. Bitsy whispered to Lucy a barely audible "thank you," as she let her slip the items into her hands. Clutching the food, she ducked beneath the ragged grey blanket to the cold outside. "I hate that blanket," she whispered into the night.

Climbing the hill to the barn she approached the side door, listening and watching. All was quiet as she inched the heavy door open. But then there he was.

It wasn't really a surprise to see Herbert Wickerson standing in the shadows of one of the carriages smoking the pipe that she was sure was forbidden to him. She smelled the burning odor of tobacco before she actually saw him and was quite sure she heard the sound of someone drinking from a jug. His father's whiskey more than likely.

Without a sound she pushed the door closed. Which way to go? It would be impossible to get up the ladder to her loft without him seeing her or hearing her even if she did remove her floppy boots.

Milly must know he was in there. She knew he came to the barn to smoke and drink. The entire household staff knew he stole his father's whiskey and his tobacco. Some of the staff had been beaten for the theft when Mr. Wickerson had discovered it. They could have told on the young Herbert, but it would've meant a double beating: once at the hands of the Master - who would not have believed a slave - and then once at the hands of Herbert himself for revealing it was him. The house slaves and servants found it easiest to just keep quiet and take the lashes that the master meted out for the theft.

Bitsy turned and crept back out the door. She moved in silence down the path to the shelter of the spreading branches of a gnarled old oak. It would be safest until he left. The tree was so huge that she could easily stay concealed. From this vantage point she would be able to see when the young master departed from his evening escapade.

Clearing a space of the hard little acorns that threatened to poke through her backside, she huddled at the base of the tree wishing she had her scrap of blanket to curl up in. The coolness of the night air began to penetrate through to her very bones. The exhaustion she felt from a full day of work began to consume her. As freezing and as uncomfortable as she was, sleep began to overtake her. She meant to close her eyes for only a moment.

The moon rose in the night sky tracing

shadowy patterns through the leaves of the grand old oak.

There was an odor of smoke in the air. It became more intense, penetrating her unconscious mind but failed to rouse her. She slept on, an uncomfortable peace surrounding her.

"...scarce any thing but Indian Corn"
Letter, 1756

The horses. Something was wrong!

Their frantic whinnying was cutting through the dark silence of the night. The crashing of their hooves on the wood walls pierced the stillness. It brought her back to consciousness. She had been dreaming of Destiny back in England and how she had ridden him out over the fields, his hooves pounding on the earth, her hair blown free of its tight bun, wildly streaming out in the wind.

But what was she hearing now?

She tried to rouse herself from the deep sleep she'd fallen into. "Oh, good Lord! What's happened?"

Rubbing at her eyes, she looked towards the barn. It was brilliantly silhouetted against the blackness of the night sky.

It was a roaring inferno.

Long, hungry flames were shooting out from between the weathered boards. And was that the shadow of a man running, outlined against the brilliant colors of the spreading flames? The horses were wild with fright.

Her feet did not touch the ground as she raced to the burning building. She lifted the heavy beam that secured the huge doors – the doors where the horses were led in and out. Pulling with all her strength she heaved the doors wide open.

The sudden whoosh of air further fueled the blaze. The horses were screaming in terror. Racing down the length of the barn she darted from one side to the other as she released the latches on the stall doors. Splinters pierced her hands as she yanked them open.

The horses, wild with panic and confused beyond reason, stampeded first towards the inferno then wheeling around, out towards the open doors. Deftly she dodged between the frantic animals. The heat from the wild flames was forcing her back.

The loft! The loft was on fire.

"Oh no." Her mind did not want to accept what she was seeing. She froze, watching the flames consume the loft. "Milly, Milly," she screamed. For just a moment she thought she saw a figure kneeling in the flames. No, it couldn't be. "Milly quick, Milly where are you?"

She was shrieking, taking in the horror of the crackling flames that were burning what was once her home. The heat was unbearable, the crackling sound deafening.

Unable to see, hardly able to breathe, she tried to find an opening to get to the ladder, but the roaring blaze had already reached the only way up to the loft. The rungs of the ladder, burning brightly, were dropping crazily into the flames. The smoke, the sound, the heat, the brilliance from the flames – how could this happen?

"Milly where are you?" she shrieked into the inferno.

The horses were wild, their screaming in panic terrifying. She was choking on the smoke. Bitsy dodged the pounding hooves of the escaping horses. Four more stalls to open.

The loft was gone. It was dropping in flaming pieces into the blistering inferno below where there had once been four elegant and ready carriages.

Brushing at her eyes, she tried to see through the smoke, thick and black, she gasped, barely able to breathe. The heat was intense. Reaching out blindly, she forced the last two stall doors open, the hinges burning her hands.

The heat singed her eyebrows, the air thick with smoke made it impossible to catch her breath.

Thunder, his eyes wide with panic was backed into the corner of his stall, his hooves flying wildly trying to fight off the threatening blaze. The flames were a hot roaring mass. They shot out and licked at, then singed Bitsy's short ring of curls. She felt the fire's heat at the hem of her thin cotton shift. Beyond the point of reason and fearing nothing at all, she entered the wild horse's stall.

"C'mon Thunder. C'mon boy, you'll be fine. It's me. I'll get you out. C'mon now." She tried to calm her voice.

Thunder, wild and unseeing, pawed the air and screamed an unnatural whinny. Bitsy slid along the edge of the stall beside the huge animal, flames threatening to cut her off, smoke choking her, closing off her throat. Easing up alongside the horse, she grabbed a handful of his mane, and yanked hard.

"Thunder, stop," she sobbed. Pulling with a strength she did not know she had, she dragged him towards the opening. Bucking and stomping and pawing the air and objecting to everything that was going on around him he fought but allowed himself to be pulled to the door of his stall.

Raising his head high he caught a whiff of fresh air and wildly headed to the beckoning doors. His hooves left deep imprints in the hard packed dirt. It took but a moment to burst forth to the fresh air and his freedom.

There was one more stall, but it was already engulfed in flames. With no strength left, slowly, unnoticed, Bitsy slid down the splintering wall amidst the choking smoke and intense heat and wild confusion.

Blissful unconsciousness washed over her as she sprawled on the hay strewn floor, flames seared the soles of her over-large, cracked leather boots. The air was deceivingly warm.

"O Dear Father..."
Letter, 1756

It was the early days of winter, 1756. The frigid iciness was setting in early. Earlier than anyone could remember. The autumn leaves were long past with their riot of brilliant mixed colors. Everyone said it was going to be a harsh winter. The squirrels were busier than usual gathering their nuts. The fat crunchy acorns had been dropping for weeks. The woolly caterpillar's black bands had been unusually wide, all pointing to an early and severe winter.

Bitsy slowly raised herself to a sitting position on the straw pallet. She listened for a moment to the cold rain hitting the sides of Lucy's cabin. Carefully getting to her feet, she tried to ignore the pain shooting through every bone in her body. This morning she was determined to help Lucy prepare something to eat, for the little ones, meager as it was. She'd been helpless too long.

Wavering a bit, choosing her steps with care, she tottered across the room, stepping in near silence around the sleeping bodies. The pail for water was near the door. Lucy was busy with her own thoughts as she poked at the morning fire.

Holding back the nearly shredded blanket, she stepped outside into the quietness of the early morning. With a quiet determination, while favoring the blistered soles of her bare feet, she went to the well, the white mist parting before her.

Her eyes, betraying her, traveled up the hill to the scene she never wanted to see again. Try as she might she couldn't ignore it. The smoky smell of the skeleton of the barn still hung heavy in the air. She stared, once again in disbelief. The blackened timbers were poking their charcoal fingers to the heavens almost as if reaching out or pleading - for what; she thought. In the spring, they said, they'd clean it up and build new. And while the days dragged by it was there to haunt her.

Tying the bucket to the rope she dropped it down into the well. It plopped against the water. Pulling the filled bucket back to the surface, her hands bandaged with rags objected to the pressure put on them.

This was where she and Milly had first been

able to talk after she'd become part of the household. Tears came to Bitsy's eyes. Her friend. She'd never been found. The fire was so hot there'd been little left. Even the metal on the carriages had melted and was found in twisted and unrecognizable shapes. Only a few of the charred timbers that had once framed the building remained upright, reaching to the heavens. A reminder to everyone of what had happened.

"Milly," she said, "maybe I didn't see you. Maybe that wasn't you that I thought I saw kneeling in the flames. Maybe you escaped." Tears ran down her pale cheeks, dripping onto the front of her light cotton shift, she swiped at them angrily. "I've got to get back." She hauled the heavy bucket of water out of the well. Holding it carefully so as not to reopen the wounds on her burned hands, her bare feet slipped and slid in the damp grass down the path to Lucy's cabin.

"Ah Bitsy, you shouldna' be doin' that yet. You jus' now gettin' yo'self back together, you jus' take yer ease a few mo' days. Then we git you back to work."

Bitsy set the bucket of water down, finding herself more drained than she expected. She wanted to hug her only friend but feared being turned away.

"Lucy, we need to get you a new blanket for that door," she said trying to lighten the moment. Lucy smiled up at her from the blackened pot she'd been stirring at the fire, "An' how we gonna do that?"

"I'll think of something," said Bitsy, "and I'm going to try to help more and not be such a burden to this family."

"You be jus' fine. I got no complaints. Them young'uns will help wif' the breakfast. I be due up to the main house early. They all git back some late las' night from that trip to Charleston. Hear tell dey had a right nice time what wif' their puttin' off that trip to England and all 'cause of the accident."

"Lucy, I've told you it wasn't an accident. He was there that night. He set that fire and I don't care what he's told everyone."

"Now Bitsy, ain't no call to be takin' on so. I knows that but we sure cain't prove it. It gonna bring nuthin' but trouble down on our heads, Lord knows, if we goes an' tries explainin' it."

"I know Lucy, I know," she wiped at the curls forming around her forehead, "I won't talk about it again, I'm sorry."

"Well, I be off to the big house. You rest yo'self. You lookin' better every day. Why you got 'bout the prettiest color hair that's growin' back in dat I ever did see."

She had to smile. Lucy'd been so good to her. It was thanks to the salves and patient nursing that had kept her alive. Lucy had swabbed on ointments and herbal creams both day and night, some sweet smelling, others so vile it was difficult not to be ill, as the scent filled the room. But they could see the regrowth of skin on Bitsy's hands and arms where it had been seared by the heat and the flames. Lucy's special mix with the white pine turpentine was miraculous. It was melted with lard and honey and beeswax. With her special touch of a sprinkle of sweet-smelling verdigris it made the wounds heal quickly. The scars would no doubt be there forever, but the pain, in time, would subside. "We all got some wounds," said Lucy. "can't be helped. Most fade with time. Some be forever." There was a deep sadness in her eyes as the words were whispered into the darkened hut.

The Mistress had been down just once to look in on her. It was not her custom to ever come to the slave quarters, preferring that Louis deal with all the day-to-day problems, but she had heard of the indentured English girl and was curious why she lived in the slave's quarters.

The mud had been thick from the rain when she arrived unannounced. She chose not to go in but stayed in the small carriage. Speaking very briefly with Lucy, a promise was made to deliver whatever potions she needed to help make Bitsy well. She told Lucy she would return at some other time and said it certainly had been a good thing that her son Herbert had been there to help.

Lucy knew to hold her tongue. She had already overheard Herbert's tale of how the runaway indentured girl, Milly had set fire to the barn with a candle and that he had tried to save her, but instead only managed to save the horses. His tale had gone on to say that after coming very close to being burned alive, he had gone back and then was able to pull Bitsy to safety even though he was sure she was dead. His family had treated him like a hero and were lavish with their praise for his self-proclaimed and undeserved bravado.

In truth, Big Jim, Lucy's husband, had grabbed Bitsy and run just before the burning building collapsed. He was the one who had beat out the flames that had started to burn the hem of her cotton dress. If she hadn't had the huge leather boots on the flames most assuredly would have burned her feet, as it was, they were merely blistered.

All but one of the horses had been saved. Thunder had survived with only a singed tail. He was still a bit skittish, but they were sure he'd settle down in time.

There was nothing that could be done. The family would never believe that Herbert was responsible for setting the fire. Those who knew the truth would not be thanked for telling it. They would all have to carry that secret with them to their graves.

The morning was drizzly as Lucy and most of her family went off to their day's chores, leaving Bitsy at the cabin with only Jacob and Jeremy, the two littlest ones still at home. She gathered the breakfast bowls and cleaned them with the rushes. It took some rubbing to remove the traces of the cornmeal and sprinkling of molasses that wanted to stick to the wood worn from years of use. And then straightening the room and sweeping took almost no time.

The two little ones entertained themselves digging in the dirt in the corner. It was not difficult to keep a three- and four-year-old busy, a stick and a cup and some dirt quickly became a carriage traveling over a hilly terrain with a wild overseer in hot pursuit. The two made little "giddy up" horse sounds but rarely did they laugh. Life was serious for the two slave children. There wasn't much that they found of amusement.

As she rolled the straw filled mattress back from the floor, hard packed from endless footsteps, she was startled as the tattered grey blanket covering the door was thrown back. Bitsy looked up, her breath caught in her throat, the mattress slid from her hands; a look of alarm darkened her blue eyes. He stood there blocking out the light from outside.

"I understand your name is Bitsy," he said. His voice was deep but seemed unsure.

Straightening up with her head held high, "Yes Sir," she said, keeping the tremor out of her voice, "that's the name that they call me." He knew her name already, she was quite sure. She looked about the room, her eyes darting about searching for an escape, trying to decide if there was space for her to slip past him and out the door.

"Send these two little pick-a-ninnies out so's we can have a word in private," he said, as he slapped his riding crop against the palm of his hand.

Bitsy gritted her teeth and signaled the two little ones to go out to play.

Jacob took Jeremy's hand, his eyes as big as saucers, and ducked past the man nearly taking up the whole doorway.

"It's alright," she whispered to the boys as they passed her.

"Now Bitsy, if that's what they call you, I understand you were the one who was pulled out of the fire. You were in front of Thunder's stall. Is that correct?"

"Yes Sir," her reply almost inaudible.

"Is it possible that you released all of the other horses?"

"Save one Sir that I was unable to reach."

"Well, I believe that you and I know the truth of what happened that night." He stood, legs apart, hands held behind his back. "Am I correct in that assumption?" His riding crop slapped at the back of his leg in a rhythmic thwack, thwack.

She lifted her head higher and defiantly looked him in the eye. "Yes Sir, it was your father's pipe that you were smoking. I smelled the tobacco smoke and I saw you by the ladder.

Then later I saw you running out the side door."

"Well girl, there's no need to review the whole bloody mess. I'd like to keep that little bit of information between you and me. Would that be possible?"

"Yes Sir, I have no reason to carry it further." She bit at her lower lip, nearly drawing blood.

"Good. Then we have an understanding, do we not?"

"Yes Sir."

"We need say no more on the subject then." He tipped back on his heels as he eyed her closely. "I'm leaving for England in the morning with my family. Perhaps while I'm there there's some little trinket that you'd like me to carry back for you?"

"I have no need of trinkets, Sir," she said lifting her chin.

"What then? Some new lace handkerchiefs perhaps or maybe a pair of satin slippers?"

Bitsy almost had to laugh - lace and satin indeed. There were so many things that were needed. Where to start? What could she use to make her life more bearable? Warm clothes, a blanket, food? She pondered a moment, chewing on the corner of her lower lip. There was one thing that would surely mean the most to her.

"Sir, if you could possibly carry a letter for me."

"And who would be writing this letter?"

"I would of course," she answered.

"And you know how to write?" his eyebrows shot up in disbelief.

"Yes, of course."

"Hmmm," he mused, contemplating. "I suppose I could do that. And who would this letter be intended for?"

"My father, Sir. He needs to know where I am."

"And why doesn't your father know where you are?"

"A long story Sir, and it was all a long time ago. I would just like to inform him that I'm well."

"Curious how you don't sound like the rest of them."

"The rest of them?"

"Yes, the slaves and the other workers. Where were you educated?"

"In England Sir, but that was a long time ago and not something that I care to discuss."

"Well, fine enough then." He unclasped his hands from behind his back and held the tattered blanket at the door with his riding crop. He turned to take his leave. "Get your letter together before tomorrow and I'll see that it's delivered."

He ducked his head and went out the door.

Bitsy breathed a sigh of relief. If that was all that he wanted it was easy enough. His family wouldn't believe the word of an indentured servant even if she did want to carry the real story of the fire to them.

The remainder of the day was taken up with locating paper and then trying to obtain a quill pen. Both she was able to acquire through Lucy. The house slave had removed a sheet of the master's fine stationery from his desk and had found a newly sharpened quill pen.

Finding ink was not going to be quite so easy; the master's supply having dried from disuse. Going through the storage shed behind the kitchen, Bitsy found a jar of indigo. By mixing it with a bit of water, a splash of vinegar and adding a bit of pulverized charcoal, she would be able to come up with a good substitute for the ink she had used back in England.

There was plenty of charcoal and ash from the recent fire. Fearing that she'd miss her opportunity to hand the master's son her letter she strained her mixture through the hem of her dress. One more dark stain on her bedraggled shift wasn't going to make a difference. Before nightfall she was able to get her almost blot free letter to the kitchen and into Lucy's hands, who would see to its safe delivery.

"Lucy," she said coming in through the kitchen door, "Here it is."

"What girl? What you doin' up here." Lucy turned from her work of shaking out and then folding a great red blanket.

"Lucy, the letter. Here, I've finished it."

"Fine," she said, "they already upstairs fo' the night. I gets it to him in the mornin'. Here," she said, "take an end, gotta get this thing upstairs fo' they start lookin' fo' it."

"Why Lucy it's beautiful, wherever did it come from?" She ran her hand over the exquisite deep red, thick wool blanket.

"They gots it in Charleston I imagine." Together they folded the beautiful blanket, Bitsy running her calloused hand over the softness once again.

"Your favorite color," she said.

"I know. I wait for it to git wore out," she smiled and ran her hand over the warmth. "Here chile, give me that letter," she said holding out her free hand.

"When will you get it to him?" Bitsy asked.

"Now you stop yer worryin', I get it to him 'fore they leave."

Bitsy handed her the letter, a worried frown crossing her brow, "If you're sure."

"I be sure."

A sigh escaped as she turned and headed back out into the darkness. The door closed behind her without a sound.

"Balance my former bad Conduct..."
Letter, 1756

The late fall turned into a harsh winter, as icy winds sought out every corner. The ponds and creeks had all frozen over long ago and now there was talk that the Chesapeake Bay itself would soon be frozen solid, stopping all shipping traffic.

No one could remember a winter quite like this. It would sleet and cover everything with a glistening coat of sparkling ice one day, and the next it would melt into slushy puddles and then freeze again as the darkness closed in. It was nearly impossible to walk without falling on the slippery coating that covered everything.

Rocks hit the ice that had formed overnight in the wash buckets. Young children tasked with breaking the solid crust shattered the early morning quiet. Winter dragged on.

Bitsy was losing hope. The day that the Wickerson family had left for England she had confronted Lucy about the letter. Had she gotten it into Herbert's hands? "Surely did," she'd answered.

"Did he pack it?" she'd asked.

"Don' rightly know." Lucy had answered, concentrating hard on an imaginary spot she was busy scrubbing.

Bitsy sensing something wrong pressed on. "Why don't you know?" she'd asked as Lucy turned her back to go on to other chores. Bitsy reached out and caught her arm.

Lucy turned back to her in annoyance. "He throw it in the trash." she'd said. The look of horror on Bitsy's face and tears that threatened to spill over must have loosened her tongue. "Jasmine may have took it. I ask her to but didn't see."

That was the end of the discussion. Bitsy knew how tight-lipped Lucy could be when she chose, and there wasn't a way to get more information out of her.

Jasmine was one of the two house slaves who would accompany the family to England. Rarely was she seen outside of the big house. Most times she slept on the floor outside of the master's bedroom door. She stayed through the night should she be needed for anything. But Bitsy knew this much: slaves couldn't read. It wasn't allowed. How could Jasmine possibly get the letter delivered?

Bitsy's black mood continued for weeks, she spent little time at Lucy's cabin. Life had changed. Big Jim and the three little boys were gone. Lucy had been stooped and care worn before, but now there was a drag to her step, and it was as if she'd become an old woman overnight. The impossible had happened and there was no going back.

Louis, on orders from the master, had sold six of the younger slaves. He'd rounded up the little ones while Lucy was up at the house. Big Jim was out clearing the fields of the rocks heaved up by the winter frosts.

Micah, from the James plantation, had come by to take the five young ones to Annapolis to be sold on the auction block. Louis had then disappeared for two weeks leaving Brisson, his new assistant, in charge. The where and why of it was not for Lucy and Big Jim to know. Their sons, along with three other young ones were gone with no trace.

It was a freezing day in the dead of winter when Louis had reappeared; Big Jim wasted no time confronting him. "Where they at?" he'd asked. "My sons." A cold hatred hardened his deep brown eyes. Louis had shown his yellow teeth in a smirk and said he had no idea - he hadn't been the one that had taken them down to the auction block. His only answer was that he assumed they went down into the Deep South with the rest of the chattel.

Bitsy stood, an unwilling observer, as she watched Big Jim approach Louis. His massive shoulders hunched over, he looked like an enraged bull about to charge.

"Now wait a minute Jim," said Louis, holding out a hand as if trying to ward him off. "T'weren't my fault. Tol' you all that. The Massa said to get rid of some of them young 'uns." He backed up trying to get out of the way of Big Jim. "Now calm down Jim," It was as if the enraged man hadn't heard a word he'd said. "Stop now, ya' hear me," Louis said as he flicked his whip.

Jim, his massive shoulders shiny with sweat despite the coldness of the day kept moving forward. Louis backed up to the wagon, caught with no other place to go. He flicked his whip menacingly, a warning to Jim. "Stop now."

But it was too late; the big slave's massive arm shot out and with one quick and easy swipe he easily yanked the whip out of the overseer's hand. Jim lifted it high prepared to crack open the skull of the man who had sold his children. Louis reached up and snatched it. Together they struggled for control of the leather strap. Louis fumbled and then grasped at the handle and in an instant had twisted off the hard leather case. It revealed the shiny point of a knife. Bitsy gasped when she saw the glint of the metal.

"Jim," she'd screamed, but he'd already seen the weapon that had been concealed in the whip's handle.

In an instant Jim had taken hold of Louis's wrist and flipped it around turning the metal blade towards the struggling overseer. Louis caught his foot on an exposed root; he tripped. Down he went. He fell hard, impaling himself on the end of his own shiny blade.

"Jim," Bitsy screamed again, but this time she was too late. Brisson had come up, unseen behind the raging slave and smashed a log with all his strength, on the back of his unsuspecting head.

Bitsy watched as his knees crumpled and as if in slow motion he sank to the ground, blood gushing from the gash on the top of his head.

The rest was a blur. Louis staggered about holding his hand at his bloodied side, Brisson ordered the other slaves to tie Big Jim to a tree. Bitsy ran to find Lucy. She had no success and by the time she returned they had done their damage.

Brisson had done his job too well. With the help of some of the others they untied what was left of Jim. They lowered him into the bed of the wagon for the journey home.

"Lucy, what can we do," Bitsy asked, as they lowered him to the straw mattress, tears streaming down her cheeks. "Can't you fix it?"

"We bring him back," said Lucy, "but fo' what?" She shook her head as if trying to rid herself of a bad nightmare. "There ain't nuthin' can be done 'bout some wounds," she sighed, "dey jus' runs too far down. Too deep," she added.

They sat, keeping a vigil, changing the wet cloths, trying to soothe the deep gashes. Gashes that were too deep to ever be cured completely. Lucy's somber face was closed to all emotion as she bent to place yet another cool wet rag over the gaping slash marks. There was indecision in her eyes that Bitsy was sorry she'd seen.

Through the night the slave and the young girl sat side by side on the hard dirt floor. Bitsy, her knees drawn up to her chest, dozed off and on. As the dawn began to lighten the morning sky they watched as his breathing became more regular.

The days passed in a quiet blur, Lucy became distant, withdrawing into herself, having little to say to anyone. She did her job, nothing more. Big Jim would leave her soon, she knew that. He had to. There wasn't a way he could stay and not be punished further. Lucy knew she'd only have Sally left and it was as if she was afraid to even touch her or speak to her. Afraid for what was next.

Big Jim disappeared into a moonless night when he was once again able to move about. For whatever reason there was no mention of his departure. Perhaps because no one was really sure just when he slipped out and certainly no one would claim to know which direction he chose.

There were no words to help Lucy with the sorrow of her losses. Bitsy chose to stay to herself. A small temporary barn had been hastily put together to house the horses. She found it easiest to spend her nights curled up there in the one vacant stall. A pile of hay was all that she needed and with the loan of a horse blanket it was almost comfortable. The huge animals sharing the small space kept it warm. The makeshift barn was more tightly constructed then the slave quarters, and it held the heat much better than the poorly built shanties, but at times it was unbearably lonely. The sadness of missing Milly had created a deep ache.

The morning was freezing. She wanted nothing more than to stay curled up in the warm cocoon she'd made for herself. An odd rattling purr came out of the near darkness. And then something warm touched her cheek. Opening her eyes, in the shadowy light, she could just make out a shaggy grey cat who was busy sniffing her ear and then her hair before it curled up to share the warmth.

"Well good morning to you," said Bitsy to the ball of fluff. "You look just about as homeless as I am." The cat looked at her approvingly and purred even louder.

"What a very pleasant surprise. Have you come to live with me?" she asked. "There's not much to eat here but we can keep each other company." Her fingers traced through the long tangled fur. "I wonder where you came from?" she asked. "But every barn needs a good cat and I'm sure you'll do just fine." She smiled down at her new friend. "No doubt you'll find something to eat. There're enough mice here to feed an entire army of cats." Her soft, though tangled fur was a treat to run her fingers through. "I think I'll call you Kitty, if that's fine with you," said Bitsy. And they became fast friends and though Kitty usually disappeared during the day, she was always waiting for Bitsy when she returned at night, ready to be petted and cuddled.

"Kitty," she said, as she ran her fingers through the long fur, trying to sort through the many tangles of her new confident and best friend. "Something's not right. That horrid man that Louis has hired is causing more problems than Louis ever did. There's going to be more trouble." Kitty looked up at her, her soft nose touched Bitsy's chin as if to say, "I understand." She purred quietly and settled herself close by her new caretaker. It was comforting, although each night she closed her eyes thinking will this ever end?

Sleep did come more easily, with her trusting friend curled up by her side. But was this to be her life?

"… suffer here is beyond the probablility of you in England to Conceive … ?"

Letter, 1756

Louis, as the overseer, had little to do in the dead of winter, and with the family not in residence there were few tasks. He and his new friend Brisson spent most of their days drinking in Louis's shack. The slaves stayed busy with their assignments of fixing and repairing farm tools and other implements. They knew to spend their days staying out of the way.

The wound in Louis's side from the knife had never healed properly and often there was a stain of fresh blood on his shirt. When he emerged from his shack, he'd stomp around growling at anyone he saw, while flicking his whip. They could all see that his temper was close to the surface, ready to explode. His face was drawn and gaunt; his skin had taken on a dry, grey hue.

It was easy enough for Bitsy to avoid him. She had more than enough to do with endless days, that often went into the night. It wasn't difficult to keep her distance from their shack and out of view of the two bored men.

Her chores now included spending time at the main house where she helped Lucy with the unending tasks that the Mistress had left for her. The work was tiresome, with mending and scrubbing and washing most everything in the eighteen-room mansion.

One crisp day, between snowfalls, Bitsy helped take down the heavy drapes in the main house to be washed. A huge vat was brought into the yard and filled with water. A roaring fire was soon built to bring it to a rolling boil. The washing and rinsing and then wringing and hanging of the massive drapes was painful on her still healing burned hands.

When that task had been completed, an entire week was spent scrubbing floors and helping to polish the endless supply of silver. It was drudgery and it was tiring; but it was far better than working the fields.

There never seemed to be a moment of idleness. Even with the endless hours put in, the list would never be complete. Did the owners know this she wondered?

There was one assignment that she enjoyed and that she could do when she wasn't helping

Lucy, and that was to make more baskets. No matter how many they made, it was never enough. Instructions were sketchy but Lucy had done her best to show her how they were woven with the damp reeds.

Bitsy found it was easier to devise her own method, which was quicker and although it didn't create as tight a weave as Lucy's, they were adequate. Once learned, it was easy enough to make them out of all the grasses and reeds that had been collected and hung to dry during the fall. And thanks to Lucy's potions, her hands were healing from the burns as once again they begun to build up enough calluses to make her chores not quite so painful.

"Kitty, come along, today we get to sit in the sun," she said. "We can make our baskets out there." She rubbed at her hollow stomach. She hardly noticed anymore that the food she'd been eating wasn't fit for the hogs. Mornings she'd reach into the bin holding the corn and as she passed out dried ears for the horses, she'd chew on one herself. Her stomach wanted to rebel but that's all there was. Today she brought out two ears to chew on while she worked at weaving new baskets.

It was quick and easy work, and she enjoyed

the small creations that she made with the reed that she kept damp and pliable in the bucket. Louis would leave her alone as long as he saw her working. When he brought the food for the week down to the slave quarters, he always begrudgingly made sure that there was a pile for her no matter how meager. There was never enough for anyone and if the grumbling that went on was true, Louis took most of the food for himself and his friend Brisson.

Bitsy sat with her back to the hastily constructed barn. The scent of the newly milled planks wafted through the air. It overpowered the charcoal odor from the burned remains. The sun felt warm even though there were dark clouds gathering on the horizon. Kitty curled up next to her. She was grateful for the warmth on a January day.

"Bitsy," she looked up startled, all her attention had been focused on weaving a useable basket. She hadn't noticed anyone approaching. Sally was standing in front of her. "I got nuthin' to do," she said shyly, her face turned to try to conceal the hot pink scar. "Wanted to take a nap but momma says no, g'wan outside." She smiled down at Bitsy, the jagged scar pulling at one side of her mouth.

"Well, Sally, you can certainly work here with me." She knew Lucy would be pleased if she taught her only daughter how to weave the reed. It could well be what would bring her up to being a house slave and not one of the field hands.

"Nah," she said toying with the end of her short black braid, boredom evident in her voice. "Don' wanna do that', I go walkin', go see them hosses."

"That's wonderful. You like them as much as I do, don't you?" Sally smiled shyly. "Well, I hope someday you get to ride one. I just know you'd love it."

"You ever have a hoss?"

"Yes, I did," she said turning back to her basket, "but it was long ago."

"You ever gonna get one again?" she asked.

"Maybe someday," she answered. "Once upon a time I was hoping to be mistress of a home in England, where I'd own lots and lots of horses and lots of land with rolling hills and forests..." her voice trailed off.

"Where's it at?" she asked.

"Oh, it's a place far away." said Bitsy, "Something out of a dream I guess."

Sally shuffled her feet in awkwardness, "I be goin' now,'" she said and turned abruptly and headed down the hill. Bitsy watched her as she half skipped, and half walked down towards the horse's pen. She was all that Lucy had left now with her boys gone and Big Jim having run away. No doubt in search of those boys thought Bitsy, but it wasn't spoken of.

Bitsy watched as Sally pulled out small clumps of grass as she went along, a treat to tempt the horses with. Turning back to her basket, she picked up a long piece of wet reed and continued to weave, hoping to finish while the sun was still warm. Hearing one of the horses whinnying she looked up to see if Sally had had any luck luring them over. She was surprised and annoyed to see Louis at the other side of the pen. His reputation for teasing and annoying the animals was well known. All the horses on the estate shied away from him. He didn't like them, and they didn't like him.

Bitsy watched as he picked up a small pebble and flung it at Thunder's haunches. She could see him smile as the big horse reared up on his hind legs and pawed at the air. But where was Sally? Gasping in horror, she saw Sally crouching down below the bottom rail to get inside the horse's pen. Thunder had panicked, the shock of the pebble had stung his hind quarters.

Even at a distance she could see the whites of his eyes, large in anger or terror, at the wound to his flank. Louis, laughing at the sport he was having, flung another pebble, this time hitting Rupert, the old grey gelding. He too reared up as though stung. His hooves pawed the air, he whinnied wildly and then started off on a mad dash around the inside of the pen, his hooves making sharp indentations in the hard packed dirt as he kicked up clods of the dark earth.

A lone crow rose from his perch in the bare branches of the maple tree cawing furiously at the disturbance below. Bitsy rose. The basket, unfinished with reeds sticking in every direction fell to the ground. She wiped her damp hands on her dress as she watched the drama that was playing out way down in the field. She began to walk fast in the direction of the pen, her oversized boots slowing her progress. Bending in the damp grass she pulled them off and threw them aside. Grabbing the hem of her ragged dress, exposing her long and too thin legs, she set off at a run.

"Sally," she screamed. "Sally, watch out." She was too late, and she knew it. Running faster, she was afraid to look but afraid not to. "Sally," she screamed again as she watched the hooves of the mighty plow horse crash down on the child.

She sped faster, leaping over clumps of dead grass, her feet barely touching the icy blades. It took only moments to run the distance but when she arrived, there was only a crumpled heap on the side of the pen. Rupert was pacing nervously back and forth along the fence, snorting, and pawing at the ground. Louis was nowhere to be seen.

It took moments only to slip under the fence, unnoticed by the two agitated horses. "Sally," she cried, stooping down next to the crumpled form. "Sally, please," tears hung on her lashes. "Please speak to me." She looked down at the too small ten-year-old, blood on her smashed leg. There was no time. The horses were agitated, not sure of the source of their stinging hunches, but moving towards the two girls, their hooves kicking up dirt. Bitsy moved quickly. She had to get her out of there. She lifted the small bundle, surprised at how she weighted almost nothing. The horses, unsure of what had stung their haunches, were moving ever closer. Holding her small bundle close she ducked down with her load and slipped under the wood rail as the horses nervous pacing brought them dangerously close.

Staggering slightly, she carried the small bundle over to a great magnolia tree. With great care she laid her burden down. "Please wake up child." She rubbed at her arm. "Wait, I'll go find someone," she said to the lifeless girl. "I can't tell Lucy. I can't do it," a sob caught in her throat. "I'll be back," she reached out a trembling hand and patted the little lifeless body. There was no breath left in the little body.

Wiping the tears blurring her eyes, with shoulders shaking with sobs, she went in search of someone to help.

Her feet felt like lead as she walked back towards the horse's pen. The day had changed. From the earlier warmth of the sun to a chill wafting through the air. It was near noon and the sun was gone; clouds were hanging heavy in the sky. There was the threat of a late winter storm. An occasional frozen flake, like a warning, blew through the air. Bitsy felt the iciness in her feet.

There was no one to be found. The big house was empty. The slave quarters were vacant.

Sure, that Sally had taken her last breath she stopped to find her boots. They sat in the long grass, an icy coating covering the hard leather. Her baskets were scattered haphazardly in the frozen blades of grass – she'd come back and gather them up later. Pulling on the freezing boots, she couldn't tell if it was colder with them on or just walking barefoot.

Her feet felt as though they were encased in icy mud as she made her way down the hill to the huge magnolia tree. She was going to have to carry Sally back to her mother. What would she tell Lucy?

Stooping below the heavy branches, she walked around the thick trunk. Sally wasn't there! It hadn't been more than minutes since she'd left to find help. How could this be? She looked around more carefully. There was disturbed soil and a smattering of bright red blood on the dead leaves, but there was no sign of Sally. There were wolves and bears in the area, but most often they stayed well-hidden during the day.

"Someone must have found her," she said aloud, tears catching in her throat.

It felt as though weights were tied to her feet as she turned in the direction they needed to go. Slowly with a despair that wanted to pull her down, she walked through the icy blades of grass back to the slave quarters.

As she rounded the corner of Lucy's cabin, she heard voices. Lucy had returned from wherever she'd been.

Bitsy stopped a moment, listening, not sure if she recognized the voice. It was Louis, talking in a tone she'd never heard him use before. Standing to one side of the tattered gray blanket she waited, not meaning to eavesdrop but unable to turn away.

"T'weren't my fault Lucy, you knows that." His voice was low, contrite, almost apologetic, no wonder she didn't recognize it. "You know I wouldn't harm your little girl. You know I always held back and never hurt her bad. But I couldn't treat her different, people'd know."

Lucy's voice, quiet, threatening, like the low growl coming from a badly disturbed mother bear hissed out, "You got it all now, ain't you. First my boys, then my man, then my only girl. You never was happy wif my havin' family, you havin' none o' yer own, was you." It was a statement, not a question.

"Look here Lucy, I done right by them three baby boys of your'n. Massa said I had to sell some of them young uns' while he be gone. That's what he said. There be too many here to feed. He jus' plain runnin' out of money. I make sure they go down to a good place. Told Micah, find a good massa for them boys and keep 'em together."

"But why? Why my boys? They be yer own flesh an' blood. You forgettin' that?"

Bitsy gasped audibly, her hand involuntarily went up to cover her mouth. She hoped they hadn't heard her. They ignored her if they did.

"Now," she continued, "there be my girl." A sob caught in her throat. "Look what you gone and done to her."

"Louis," she cleared her throat, her voice becoming stronger, "I'm gonna kill you." Her voice rose, the grief nearly screaming through. "If we wasn't twins, born of da' same mother, I'd a' done it long ago. My Jim talk of it many a time, of how you could meet wif an accident an' we be done wif you. But I says no, cain't kill my own flesh. Now look! Look what's happened. Whyn't, I let him, then' he still be here."

"Lucy, I done tol' you, I be sorry."

"Sorry ain't gonna bring my family back. You git outta my sight now. I don' never wanna lay eyes on da' likes o' you again. Long as I take a breath you better not cross my path."

"But Lucy..."

"Git out!" she cried. "Git outta my sight."

Bitsy heard rustling as if there was a scuffle

and was nearly knocked over as a grim Louis hastily backed out of the hut. He turned and ran down the path. Lucy stood in the doorway, holding back the gray blanket with one hand and in the other the metal rod she used to poke at the fire.

Bitsy looked at the dark woman. She'd never seen such a look of hatred and loathing. Peering around Lucy, she caught just a glimpse of the child lying on the straw mattress, her leg at an odd angle.

"I'm sorry, Lucy. I'm so sorry." Tears coursed unchecked down her cheeks. Lucy merely nodded, then turned and pushing aside the grey rag that served as a door, went back into her hut as the child began to whimper.

"kindle up that flame..."
Letter, 1756

"Lucy, I can't stay here. I have to leave. I don't care if they kill me. I don't care if they find me again. I'm so hungry and I'm so cold and I'm so worn, anything is better than this." She stood in front of Lucy, shivering, her dress in rags, one hand rubbing unconsciously at her empty stomach.

"You said they'd bring me up to the main house to work, well they're not going to do that. They're going to send me back out to the fields as soon as they return and I'm going to die anyway. I may as well die trying to gain my freedom. I can't live this way any longer." She wiped angrily at a tear that had escaped down her flushed cheek.

"I shall try to get word to my father again to see if he still doesn't want me. Whatever happens I'm sure I'll never see England again," she continued as she swiped at the tears. "Either starvation is going to get me or Brisson's whip will do the job. I've got to go. You can come with me if you like," she said reaching out her hand to touch Lucy's sinewy arm.

"Gonna stay right here. What if my boys come back, try to find me? Gotta be here if they come lookin'."

"Are you sure, Lucy? You know Louis is probably going to kill you too!"

"No, he ain't gonna go killin' me too," she said matter of factly. "Some days I wish to God he would." She seemed to stand a little taller. "He goin' anyways – you wait and see. He not stayin' here much longer."

"Why is he afraid of you, Lucy? He always seems to stay far away from you."

"Didn't know he stayed away from me," she said.

"How can you stay here?" Bitsy asked.

"Told you. Gotta. Gotta wait for my three boys and my Jim. They's all comin' back one day."

"Lucy, this can't be. I wish you'd come with me."

"Cain't and that's an end to it."

"Then Lucy, I'm going to miss you, but I've got to leave, I can't stay here another day," she said, as she turned to leave. "If you change your mind, come and find me." Turning back, she hugged her, tears welling up in her eyes.

"G'wan now," said Lucy. "Massa due home tomorrow, you go on and git 'fore they all gits back here."

Bitsy ducked out beneath the grey blanket that was now nothing more than a few strips of faded thin wool. She turned in the direction of the big house. There was a mission she needed to take care of before she left.

A shiver ran up her spine as she let herself in. The house was cold and empty and unwelcoming. First, she stopped at the huge desk that held all the master's papers and accounts and pens. Opening the small bottle of what was left of the ink, she sat in the big chair usually occupied by the owner of the plantation. It felt good if not a bit awkward.

Dipping the quill pen in the bit of ink, she composed her letter. It would be brief, knowing there was no need to rehash how the barn had been burned down and all about his son and all about Milly. But she wrote about who she was, with a minimum of explanation and then wrote about Lucy, her three sons and Big Jim. She wrote that consideration should be extended to them explaining that every effort should be made to reunite them. There was little sense in explaining they were quite possibly kin to the master as chances were that he already knew that. And all this before the ink ran dry!

Bitsy went up the winding stairs: her booted feet slapped on the oriental runner that led the way to the second floor. Memories of home washed over her, the feel of the smooth banister beneath her hand all too familiar.

Walking quickly, her clip clopping steps muffled by the thick carpeting, she found her way to the far end of the hall. She stood for just a moment in front of the polished wood doors admiring the intricate carving. She pushed the two heavy double doors open to expose a darkened room. It was cold and sterile, the empty hearth unused all these weeks. Slowly, deliberately, she walked around the room, her fingers tracing patterns in the fine coating of dust covering the windowsills. The bed, cold, regal, imposing and unslept in was pushed tightly against the wall. The rich damask coverlet, a few almost unseen tears at the hem, covered the massive bed, hiding what was underneath.

Bitsy moved quickly. Slipping out of her dirty, cracked, boots, she set them neatly at the side of the bed, there would be no mistake as to who had been here. Tucking the letter she had written into the boot, she smiled as she removed her prize, tucked it under her arm and slid silently out the door, pleased that there had been enough ink left to add the p.s. as to who was responsible for the theft of the red blanket.

The crescent moon had risen, casting a muted light from behind the dark thin clouds that were threatening to blot it out. Bitsy, shed of the heavy boots, strode down the hill, her head held high, the rolled-up prize on her shoulder. She had gone out of her way to use the wide curving path that led from the sprawling mansion to the road. The tree lined drive brought guests and carriages up to the main house. Walking the hard packed drive was something the slaves were never allowed to do. But here it was. A last gesture to her freedom.

The hour was late. The lone dog that so often announced the comings and goings in the slave quarter ignored the familiar step. She strode determinedly to Lucy's door, knowing the exhausted slave slept the sleep of the dead.

The muted light from the waning moon guided her as she effortlessly pulled down what was left of the tattered grey fabric. Working in near silence, she tucked her prize up under the loose boards, catching it on the splintery doorjamb. It was too wide, but the length was about right.

"There you go. And your favorite color," she whispered into the night air as she stood back a moment to admire her work. "Looks fine to me," she said.

The new red blanket covering the door replaced the one that had hung there entirely too long. It nearly glowed with its brilliance in the moonlight. Bitsy smiled. A warm feeling of satisfaction crept over her as she turned and made her way, for the last time, down the dirt path, where the footsteps of so many others had gone before.

" ... *pity your Destress Daughter...*"
Letter, 1756

It was easy. So easy she wondered why she hadn't done it long ago. She just walked down the path; as simple as that, putting one foot in front of the other as she moved further away from the ugliness, the cold, the starvation, and the misery. The pale-yellow glow from the moon lit her way. Boldly, bravely, she went down the well-trodden route. There was no one about to stop her.

The dappled moonlight filtering through the bare branches cast long shadows. Without pausing she passed the two stately brick columns that marked the end of the lane to the main house. The weeds, unchecked, hid the crumbling brick at the base of each of the wide columns. Not bothering to turn for a last look she continued down the middle of the lane, thankful for the pale light of the moon.

She would head for Annapolis, or Providence, or even Boston. She could find work somehow, she didn't even care what she did, anything was better than the life she'd been forced into.

As the night wore on the freezing rain that had held off began in earnest, quickly soaking her through. Her teeth chattered as the morning began to lighten. Without her boots, her feet were near frozen, and she'd eaten the last of the corn. She would need to find shelter soon or risk dying in some ice-covered field.

The eastern sky showed hope of an early dawn. And could it be? Far off in the distance, there appeared to be a farm. If only she could make it! There would be some shelter from the dastardly weather.

Cutting across a field thick with winter rye, she approached the darkened barn. Without a sound she slipped through the side door and looked for a pile of hay to burrow into. The cows barely noticed; one looked over at her and then returned to chewing her cud. The barn felt warm and safe and there was, she was sure, little chance of being discovered. Tiredness and hunger washed over her, the tiredness claiming her first.

Vaguely she remembered hearing the sounds of the farmer coming in to milk the cows, then listened, her mind cloudy with sleep, as he shooed them out the door.

The hours slipped by as she slept on. The bang of the barn doors as they were thrown open woke her from her deep but troubled sleep. It was the end of the day. She was surprised at the hour as she listened to the farmer bringing back his herd. Hungry now to the point of starvation she stayed hidden in the deep hay waiting for the farmer to settle his cows for the night.

The minutes ticked by as she felt the hollowness of her stomach getting deeper. When she heard the farmer let himself out and drop the bolt across the doors she emerged from her hiding place. With hands shaking from hunger, she took a pail and squeezed a bit of milk from one of the reluctant cows.

Feeling the hands of a stranger and an inexperienced one at that, the brown and white cow kicked out at the unknown person, but Bitsy, determined, squeezed out a cup of warm foamy milk. It was all that was left from the cow that had so recently been relieved of her bounty.

In minutes the starving young girl had consumed it all and thought about more. Sure that her stomach would rebel, she instead let herself out to continue on her way. Passing the winter's supply of dried corn kept for the animals she reached into the corncrib and helped herself to a few ears.

The moon had risen, and the stars were twinkling in the icy night. Her instincts told her to continue heading east.

The iciness on her bare feet was painful but she knew if she kept moving, she would warm up a bit. The borrowed blanket offered some protection from the night air. A twig snapped behind her; turning quickly she thought she saw the silhouette of a dark figure ducking behind a tree. Her eyes, she was sure, were playing tricks on her. She stood and listened for a moment but heard only the far-off caw of a wakeful crow and the rattling of the dead leaves of a black oak, disturbed by a quiet breeze. Turning, all her senses on the alert, she continued her journey.

Again, she was sure there was something behind her. She'd heard of Indians in the area, but she'd never seen one, and there were certainly bears but they should be hibernating during the cold weather. Nevertheless, she picked up her pace.

Just ahead there was a wide expanse of what appeared to be an open field covered with a fine coating of icy whiteness washed in the glare of the moonlight. She would have to move quickly if someone or something was in fact following her. Stopping for a moment she judged how far it would be to cross the open field.

The distance could be covered quickly if she ran fast. The tree line on the other side would help her to disappear. If her near frozen feet co-operated, she would make it in little time. There were no sounds behind her; the night was almost still with only the sound of water gurgling off in the distance - no doubt coming from a far-off stream.

Get ready, she said to herself. "Go," Her feet, although they felt like frozen stumps, obeyed her command as she set off in a sprint across the wide expanse of white nothingness. There was running behind her, she was sure of it. But not daring to turn, she sprinted even faster.

A sudden loud crack. Like a gunshot. It split the night air. The icy ground beneath her feet trembled. In but a split second she knew. She was on the ice covering a river or a pond. This was not a field. The ice was cracking. The instant she realized what had happened it gave way beneath her feet. She was plunged into a freezing blackness. The cold numbed her body in seconds, her arms froze stiff, she couldn't lift them, it was as if they were separate from her body.

The freezing water sucked her down, beneath the ice. There was no help. She was drowning. Was this to be her end? The thought vaguely floated through her mind as she slipped into nothingness.

"... too well knowing of your care a nd tenderness for me..."
Letter, 1756

They'd had to bury him out back. Back be-hind the barn. He had dragged her through the icy night, the farmer said, then collapsed him-self. Mrs. McGregor the farmer's wife had been so kind to her, bringing her warm drinks and setting her bed close to the fire to get every bit of warmth.

"He said he was accompanying you to Bal-timore when you both fell through the ice. I'm sorry he didn't survive, but with that festering wound in his side and the freezing water, then trying to get you back to help, it wasn't possi-ble," said Mrs. McGregor almost apologetically. Her English was impeccable although she and her husband had only recently arrived from No-va Scotia.

Bitsy stared into the flickering flames on the hearth incredulous that it must have been Louis who had saved her. Saved her why, and for what, she had to wonder. But he had pulled her out of the icy waters and then dragged her across a wide field to a lonely farm. It was more than she could fathom.

"My husband takes the wagon in to Baltimore now and again to get supplies. He'd be glad to carry you in to complete your journey."

"Thank you, Mrs. McGregor, I would indeed like that very much."

The plump, friendly woman chattered on, never lacking for things to talk about. Having only recently emigrated from Canada they were both more than thrilled to have settled in Maryland. They had laid claim to land just west of Baltimore and had hopes of planting tobacco in the spring. Their home and barn hadn't been completed but Mr. McGregor worked on one or the other almost daily. Hammering echoed through the house for most of the day.

Time passed pleasantly in the warmth of the farmhouse. There was plenty to eat and they were happy to share. Bitsy was nearly well. For a brief moment she thought perhaps she should stay right where she was. Mrs. McGregor had told her more than once that she was welcome to stay for as long as she liked. She could certainly help with all the farm work. Perhaps though there would be more opportunity for employment in one of the nearby cities. The decision was made.

Mr. McGregor was ready to make his trip into town for supplies and she knew it was time to move on.

"I'm reluctant to leave, Mrs. McGregor, you've been so kind."

"Well now child, you know you're welcome to stay," she said as she reached up to give her young charge a big affectionate bear hug. "And this," she said, handing Bitsy a leather pouch, "was on the colored fellow. Louis did you call him?"

"Yes, that was his name."

"Well, we found this strapped to his belt. Don't know as he has any kin so we'll just hand it over to you and you may do with it as you see fit." She gave her another hug, then tucked a warm blanket around her. "Goodbye now Bitsy," she said, "I shall miss you greatly."

"Thank you again for all you've done," she said, leaning down from the farm wagon and taking the offered leather purse, "I will never forget you both and your kindness to me."

The day was brilliantly sunshiny and warm as they plodded along the country roads. Bitsy was quickly bored by the silence of the quiet farmer; his wife had done all the talking, enough for both. Although his English was quite good, he preferred his native Gaelic in conversing with anyone. Bitsy knew just a bit of the language as some of the household staff back in England had been from Scotland, but she hadn't let on, not sure of who she could trust.

Fingering the leather purse, all that remained of Louis, she wondered just what she should do with it. The scent of tobacco still clung to it. Her first thought was to either burn it or throw it out, sure that no good would ever come from anything he possessed. The leather was hard, almost crisp from being soaked and then dried. She'd need to open it, much as she didn't want to. Maybe then burn whatever was in it and be done with him.

The flap cracked as Bitsy folded it back. Bits of tobacco spilled out as she spread the contents on the woolen blanket tucked around her knees. There was a sizeable collection of folded money. "There's enough here to buy Lucy's freedom," she said. The farmer politely looked at her and smiled.

"Lucy?" he said.

"Yes, she's his sister, twin sister actually," she mused. The farmer nodded and then turned his attention back to the horses, flicking the reins on the rumps of the two patient animals.

Bitsy turned her attention back to the pile on her lap. Other than the money there was a folded piece of paper that seemed to have only gotten a little damp and was now dried. Carefully she unfolded it. For just a moment she thought maybe it was the paper that the nearly blind man in the carriage had handed him weeks ago. Louis couldn't read so had tucked it away.

Carefully she unfolded it. It was a reward poster. Afraid of what it would say, she shied away from the farmer, hoping he couldn't read or if he could, wouldn't attempt to. Her eyes widened as she saw her name blazoned in big bold letters across the top of the tattered paper. Tears started to blur her eyes making it difficult to read the faded print.

"REWARD" it said just below her name.

"£50 POUNDS STERLING." A sizeable sum, she thought for an unskilled indentured servant. That amount would buy more than enough able bodied slaves! She wanted to laugh out loud. Who would pay a sum like that for an insignificant runaway? The tears were blurring her vision.

With a price like that on her head it was going to be hard to hide and how did anyone know she'd end up as a runaway? She read further: *"Tall, thin, English girl, gold colored hair, educated, 16 years old. Mistakenly sold into indenture."*

Tears were dripping on the already blotted words. "Mistakenly! Mistakenly," she said out loud. "Mistakenly," she said again, incredulously. The farmer began to eye her with some trepidation. "Here look," she said. "It says mistakenly." She wiped at the tears with the sleeve of her dress, trying to clear her vision.

"Anyone knowing the whereabouts of this young girl contact Samuel Goldstein, Barrister, Baltimore, Maryland, acting agent for Charles Edward Sprigs, Esq.

"That's him," she gasped, grabbing the unsuspecting farmer's arm. "That's my father. See! See!" she said holding out the poster. "That's my father."

"And so, Miss Sprigs, we will have you on the ship sailing for England in the morning. I can tell you there'll be one very happy father when he sees you."

He adjusted his spectacles and spread his long-fingered hands on the mahogany desk, polished to a hard, but warm brilliance.

Bitsy smiled. The damask covered chair comfortably enveloped her. New kid gloves covered tired hands. Gloves that would give those hands time to heal the many hidden wounds.

It had been a week since the farmer had delivered her to the door of Samuel Goldstein, Barrister, in Baltimore. He had walked her up the stairs and into the office of the barrister as she'd been shaking so badly, he was afraid she wouldn't be able to climb the stairs.

He stayed for the initial questioning of the young girl, verifying what he knew and listening as Bitsy answered the inquiries about her former life in England. Bitsy hugged him as he said his goodbyes.

Tears were close to flowing. She took a deep breath and sat again, across from the barrister.

Mr. Goldstein knew she was the one they'd been searching for.

"How did my father know where to look?" she asked smoothing an imaginary wrinkle out of her new beige silk dress.

"He didn't." Folding his hands, he continued. "He said he received a letter from you, which had been found in a hotel room in London, probably left by one of the guests."

"It was only recently that the hotel had the

letter delivered to him." The barrister let out a great sigh. "It can only be imagined how upset he was on learning your fate."

"The letter," she said, wiping at a lone tear. "The one I wrote."

He paused and then continued. "He apparently questioned the entire household staff and was able to determine that Foster, he was the gardener you remember, was involved. He sent for him and was told that he'd been instructed," and here he paused for a moment, "by your stepmother, to put you on the next ship sailing to the Colonies."

The young girl wiped at a tear with her new linen handkerchief. The barrister continued. "Earlier he had this poster printed. It was distributed up and down the east coast. He was here months ago. He'd gone to most of the large plantations in the area, but no one knew anything."

"And my stepmother?" she asked.

"Well, she and her daughter, Guinevere, is it? They no longer reside at the estate. Your father thought it best if Guinevere go away to school and your stepmother has gone back to London."

"Well thank you then Mr. Goldstein," she said rising, "I'm anxious to be getting on that ship in the morning." He rose also and hastened to help her with her new green wool cape.

"It's been my pleasure," he said, taking her extended hand. "I will see to it that your friend Lucy gains her freedom with the money you've given me from her brother, and I'll see to it that she gets whatever remains. And I will certainly make myself available if I can be of assistance in finding her children or her husband."

"And don't forget the red dress." She smiled. "It's her favorite color."

"Of course," he said bowing to the young woman.

"Thank you then," said Bitsy, "I will be counting the hours until I can be reunited with my father."

He smiled and held the door as the tall, too thin but strikingly handsome young girl passed before him.

FACTOIDS

1. Indentured servants began to arrive in America in the early 1600s. It was a concept developed to help the large landowners manage and farm their extensive acreage.

2. During the early colonial period well over one half of the immigrants to this country arrived as indentures. Most were under the age of 25. Some had been kidnapped or coerced with false promises and then sold into indenture.

3. After serving their contracted time, which could be from three to five years, but varied widely, indentures were often given land or goods for their services.

4. Indentures were often not well treated. Close to 50 percent perished while serving their time, many from disease or abuse.

5. The concept of indenture began to lose popularity in the late 1700s as slavery proved more lucrative for the landowners.

6. Literacy among indentured servants was unusual. Many were unable to even sign their names, often using an "X" for a signature.

7. The landowners in the Chesapeake Bay area owned large tracts of land, many with 250 acres or more. Tobacco was the cash crop, which was primarily shipped to England.

8. Captains transporting the indentured servants to the Colonies would often own their contracts. On arrival they would sell their "cargo" to the planters or merchants, who would pay for their passage as well as other charges.

9. Africans were originally brought to the Chesapeake Bay area as indentured servants, which changed early in the 18th century.

10. The 13th Amendment, passed in 1865, abolished slavery and indenture. It wasn't until 1917 that the British government ended the practice of indenture.

BIBLIOGRAPHY

Daniels, Roger. *Coming to America: A History of Immigration and Ethnicity in American Life*. 1991. Reprint. Perennial. New York, 2002.

deCrevecoeur, J. Hector St. John. *Letters From an American Farmer and Sketches of Eighteenth-Century America*. 1925. Reprint. Penguin Classics. New York, 1986.

Earle, Alice Morse. *Home Life in Colonial Days*. 1898. Reprint. Jonathan David Publisher. New York, 1975.

Everett, Susanne. *History of Slavery*. 1996. Reprint. Chartwell Books, Inc. Edison, N.J., 1997.

McWilliams, Jane W. *Annapolis, City on the Severn: A History*. Johns Hopkins University Press. Baltimore, 2011.

Morgan, Edmund S. *American Slavery, American Freedom*. W.W. Norton & Co. New York, 1975.

Antietam
Waking the Fury

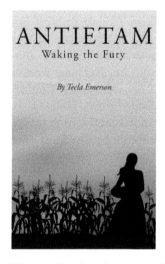

Emily at 15 is bored and annoyed with just about every-everything and everybody. Tired of her chores and irritated by the endless care of three younger sisters, she would like to have a life of her own. Her parents are absent; her Father is off fighting a war she doesn't understand and her Mother has left for Pennsylvania. As the eldest of the four sisters, she must take responsibility for her home and family. When the bloodiest battle of the Civil War is fought almost on her doorstep she is unwillingly pressed into service. Emily is called on to make decisions and to take charge of wounded soldiers while fending off the invading troops and protecting her younger sisters. Life changes forever as she discovers a courage that she did not know she possessed. Strengths emerge as she stands up for her beliefs while sheltering the enemy and caring for a runaway slave, both of which hold very serious consequences. In this remarkably accurate depiction of the Battle of Antietam, a legend is once more uncovered. It involves a mass of very angry bees. This dangerous, stinging swarm may well have had an influence on the outcome of that fateful day in 1862.

Jennie Wade
A Girl From Gettysburg

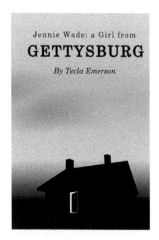

Jennie Wade: a Girl from
GETTYSBURG
By Tecla Emerson

It had been foolish to stay but now there was no choice. It was anyone's guess what the outcome would be. Nothing was as it should be. Oddly, the Confederate troops were pouring in from the north and Union troops were marching in from the south. They arrived in droves. The town was not prepared for what happened during the early days of the summer, 1863. Jennie, a young local girl, did her best to keep up with the demand for bread and water and medical care for the troops. Her brothers were scattered, her sister would soon be having a baby, her mother was not bearing up well and Jack, her intended, had not been heard from in weeks. It was a time and place that would be recorded in American history forever. A time marked by the largest number of casualties in the Civil War. It was Gettysburg, Pennsylvania, a small, unremarkable town; an easily forgotten town that would live in infamy and one that history would never forget. Of the almost 50,000 casualties of that encounter in early July, only one civilian was killed. This is her story. The story of Jennie Wade, a dedicated young woman thrown into the middle of one of Americans' most tragic times.

Mists of the Blue Ridge

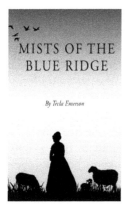

MISTS OF THE
BLUE RIDGE

By Tecla Emerson

Olivia lived a quiet and protected life tucked away on a farm in the Blue Ridge Mountains. It was far from the great war that had been raging between the North and the South. She had little interest in the who and the why of it all, and wasn't even sure where her sympathies lay. Then, without warning, the conflict surrounded her. At 16, she was ill prepared for the responsibilities that were thrust on her.

This is her story. It's a tale that tells of courage, determination and survival during one of America's most trying times.

Hidden in the Early Light
a tale of the Irish famine

Katy was 16 when the hard times came. Her father disappeared in the night and her mother left her with a tiny baby sister. She was suddenly thrust into the role of caretaker. It was a responsibility she didn't want. The farming life was not for her and now she had to find a way to survive and to keep her younger brothers from starving. How could she ever be free of a life she hadn't chosen?

It was the 1840s and thousands were dying from the great potato famine, one of history's most dreadful events.

This is Katy's story, the story of how a young girl survived by using her wits, determination and courage.

Shadows in the Fog

A Block Island Tale

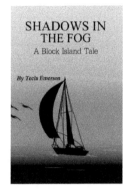

Milly lived on an island far away from the mainland. She was an orphan and there was no one to care for her. Sent to live in a house filled with boys she was pressed into the role of cook and caretaker. Her life became that of a servant.

When an unfortunate incident took place that threatened to scar her forever, she was sent to live with an angered and bitter veteran of the Civil War.

Living the life of a recluse and with battle scars of his own, he keeps his past hidden from all. Hidden until Milly comes to stay.

This is the tale of a young girl's quest for survival and how she brings herself out of the depths of despair as she learns of her mysterious past. Uplifting and compelling, the tale follows Milly as she matures and accepts all that life has given her.

Gift of the Winds
A Tale of Hendricks Head Lighthouse

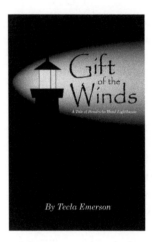

In the late 1800s a ferocious nor'easter traveled up the New England coast. It forced a three-masted schooner up on the rocks. It was within sight of the Hendricks Head Lighthouse. History says there were no survivors. However, a trunk was found that had been washed ashore. It held a most unusual and interesting surprise.

The tale unfolds through Abigail's diary. It tells of the unfortunate event that condemned her to the life of a recluse in Ireland. Life is difficult for her, but determined to survive; an inner strength takes over. Alone, she sets out for a new life in America.

Andersonville:
The Long Journey Home

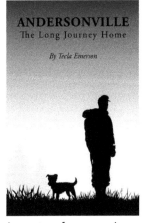

ANDERSONVILLE
The Long Journey Home

By Tecla Emerson

Hock snuck off in the dark of night to join the Union Army. He was too young to be part of the fighting force but now, taller than most, he easily joined their ranks.

Wounded in the battle at Petersburg he was captured and sent to a Confederate prisoner-of-war camp – a camp so horrid, it is still written of today. As one more of Andersonville's nameless inmates, he was given a number. Identified as "Unknown 9586," he was thrown on the death cart and hauled out as one of the dead. "Unknown 9586," did not rest in peace. Leaving the site of his burial, he set out for the north. Alone, starving, wounded and unarmed he began his journey. This is his story. From the hills of Vermont to the sights and scenes of horror that are found on battlefields and then to his final destination. It's the tale of prisoner #9586 – Unknown. The prisoner who missed his own burial.